HARD
MOUNTAIN
CLAY

PRAISE FOR
HARD MOUNTAIN CLAY
BY C.W. BLACKWELL

"Resonant and harrowing, *Hard Mountain Clay* is a haunting and visceral story of survival, betrayal, and the power of hope. Like a Californian William Gay, Blackwell writes with compassion and honesty about the worst, and the best, of human nature taking us deep into the dark to see glimmers of beauty. Raw, wrenching, and brave, *Hard Mountain Clay* will change you."

—**Meagan Lucas**, author of *Songbirds and Stray Dogs*

HARD MOUNTAIN CLAY

a novella

C.W. BLACKWELL

SHOTGUN HONEY

2023

Shotgun Honey
215 Loma Road
Charleston, WV 25314
www.ShotgunHoney.com

Cover Design by Bad Fido.

First Printing 2023.

ISBN-10: 1-956957-11-1
ISBN-13: 978-1-956957-11-2

9 8 7 6 5 4 3 2 1   23 22 21 20 19 18

for Amy, Enzo, and Miles

HARD
MOUNTAIN
CLAY

HE TOOK THE TURNS HARD.

Wheel cranked, shoulder dipped.

He leaned into it.

Lou always told us you didn't need brakes if you *knew what the fuck you were doing.* Even in a big F-250 extended cab with eighteen-inch mudders and a cable winch. He'd say a professional like him could circle the globe on a single pair of brake pads with nothing but the gearshift and his good looks to slow him down. Maisy and I joked about Lou trying to drive that big dumb truck across the Pacific Ocean, yanking the wheel through undersea canyons down there in the dark with the eels and the angler fish, holding his breath all the way to Japan in a feat of sheer pride.

We didn't joke about it to his face, though.

Never to his face.

Lou Holt blew into our lives a few months after Mama got a job waitressing at the Oak Street Diner. He drove a truck for one of the local tow companies—Speedy Tow, not Ballard's—and he'd take long-haul jobs on the side for extra cash. She'd been complaining about needing work done to the house, so he started sniffing around the place to see what he might get in return. Soon enough, he was stopping by every weekend with his tools and his truck and his simmering temper that frothed under every word he said to Maisy and me.

One day, he just never left.

Lou wasn't all bad, though. At least, not at first.

Once, he gave me a brand new harmonica.

"You're the first to put your lips on this sonofabitch," he said, taking it out of the package and holding it to the sun so the metal gleamed. Part of getting a present was doing the unwrapping yourself, but this was the kind of thing Lou did all the time. He'd take even the smallest wins for himself, as if there were only so many wins in the world and he needed to collect all he could before they ran out.

I blew a few chords into the harmonica and looked it over.

"You got it upside down, dummy," he said. "The numbers go on the top."

Mama crossed her arms whenever he called us names, but she never told him not to. Maybe she'd bat her eyelashes and give him a tight-lipped smile like *oh come on now, Lou*, but she'd never say anything. Maybe she felt like she'd run off too many men and had to choose her words carefully now. She'd take notes in her mind of all the nasty things he'd say to us and try to build us back up after he left.

I flipped the harmonica and gave it another try, but Lou snatched it from me.

"That don't sound good either," he said. "Here, do it this way." He put it to his lips and played a little riff and made a sort of *wow wow wow* sound by slapping his fingers over the back of it. It didn't sound great, but Mama was delighted. She clapped her hands and made a *wow* sound of her own.

"See that, Benny boy," she said. "If you practice, you can be that good someday."

I ended up giving the harmonica to Maisy.

We both loved music, loved staying up late listening to the radio. We didn't have MTV like the other kids, so our little Panasonic radio taught us everything about all the new bands coming out of Seattle, just a few hundred miles up the coast from us. But Maisy seemed to understand music better than I did. I'd catch her spinning the dial from one end to the other, listening to oldies and classical music, even the AM country stations. It wasn't just that she was older than me—we were only eleven months apart—she was just a little better at everything. I wasn't jealous about it either, but proud. I looked up to her. And even though the kids teased her for being skinny and frail, she looked out for me like an older sister should. So when she got good at the harmonica, I wasn't surprised at all. She'd listen to the blues programs on the college radio station and play along. She picked up a riff here and a riff there, and soon she was better than Lou. *Much better.*

While Lou was giving me things like harmonicas and pocketknives, he'd give Maisy prissy trinkets like dolls and unicorn school binders. She hated everything he ever gave her. Once, he gave her a flower identification guide that boasted over three hundred illustrations of native California wildflowers. She thumbed through the pages and glanced around the front yard. It was February and neither of us spotted any flowers around, save for a few dandelions that hung sadly in the shaggy grass. The book suddenly looked heavy in her hands. Lou read her expression and his face tightened up, jawbone grinding under that wiry black beard. He stroked his chin and flecks of dandruff sprinkled onto his shirt like ash.

Mama took the book and looked it over with a certain manufactured flourish, like she made a living selling flower books. "With all the rain we've been having, I bet flowers will be springing up all over the place." She swept her hand through the air like a gameshow model demonstrating all the prizes we could win. "Won't that be something, Maisy girl?"

Maisy shrugged. "I guess so."

"Ain't girls supposed to like flowers?" Lou said. The way he said it came with hooks, barbs, and sharp edges all at once. We could tell Lou had an accent, like something we'd heard in some old TV rerun or seventies Western flick, but he never told us where he came from. He mentioned East Texas, Tennessee, even Boca Raton. Wherever he'd come from, we wished he'd go back—*and soon.*

"I guess some do," said Maisy.

I slipped the book out of Mama's hands and flipped it open to a section on sticky monkey flowers. A bouquet of tiny orange petals filled the page.

"I like flowers," I said.

"I bet you like flowers, boy." Lou's voice was ice cold. "I bet you like them just fine."

I didn't understand what he was getting at, at least not then. But that's when I ended up trading Maisy the harmonica for the flower book. Come spring, we'd sit along the creek and she'd play sad blues riffs into her palms and I'd scoot around looking for new wildflowers to identify. I found plenty of Blue Houndstongue and forget-me-nots, some brodiaea on the hillsides. I'd pepper the stream with tiny blue petals and watch them whorl and glide out of sight, all the way to the Pacific Ocean, I guessed. Maybe it wasn't how Lou pictured it, but we didn't care. In time, those peaceful moments grew shorter and shorter as Lou took over the house. Soon we were like those little blue petals, spinning and looping in the current toward some dark and unfathomable end.

MAMA DIDN'T COME HOME on the last day of school.

I insisted we hold out until dark before eating dinner
without her. We had our little traditions that we looked
forward to when school ended, and this year marked
the end of elementary school for Maisy—and the first
year I'd attend school without her. In other years, Mama
would bake cupcakes and frost half with chocolate
frosting and half with vanilla since Maisy and I liked
them differently. Then she'd sing us a graduation song
and complain about how fast we'd grown and how old
we'd become.

Darkness came, and the house grew cold. Mama still
hadn't come home. At nine o' clock, Maisy put on a kettle, and we made instant oatmeal and scooped it up with
torn heels of white bread like crude utensils. The heels
always tasted stale, but when it came right out of the
toaster with butter, I didn't mind at all. Neither of us
wanted to be the first to ask where Mama might be, as if
saying it would make the situation worse somehow. With
the kettle still hot, we poured mugs of hot chocolate—
the Swiss kind with the little dried marshmallows—and
put on our jackets and beanies. We went out back where

the land sloped and twisted toward the creek and we sat against the old redwood we called the Grandfather tree. We called it that because Mama told us she'd buried a mason jar full of her father's ashes at the base of the tree, but she always seemed a little playful when she said it. True or not, we chose to believe it. A part of me liked that our grandfather remained with us in some way. I didn't know much about him, couldn't even remember his face. Maisy said that some parts of the house still carried his scent—like pipe tobacco and mushroom soup. She said his ghost lingered in those places, and that's why we could still smell him there.

She told a lot of ghost stories.

When things got tough, we'd try to scare each other with creepy tales of vengeful ghosts or hungry monsters from deep in the woods. Maisy's stories were much scarier than mine, but they put me at ease somehow, as if the ridiculous horrors of her imagination tamed the smaller horrors of everyday life.

"You first, Benny." She took a noisy sip from her mug and watched me through the steam, eyes narrow and serious. The night smelled like fog and wet grass, crickets chanting in the dark places. "Scare me," she said.

I put my lips to the mug, deemed it still too hot, and rested it in my lap. I thought for a moment, trying to recall some recent nightmare or anxious thought I'd gotten hung up on, but all I could think about was why Mama hadn't come home. I suddenly didn't want to tell a story.

"Mama's dead and she's not coming home again," I said. My eyes welled when I said it. "That's my story."

She squeezed closer, so we were knee-to-knee. It

7

struck me how much smaller her knees looked than mine, as if she'd quit growing two years back.

"She'll come home, little brother. It's not the first time."

"I saw her buy the cupcake mix and everything. I know she didn't forget."

"Maybe we can figure out the cupcakes together," she said. "The instructions are on the back of the box. I've seen her do it a few times. Just need a bowl and a whisk. Maybe eggs?"

"I don't care about the cupcakes, just as long as she's okay."

"She's okay, Benny. We'd know somehow if she wasn't, don't you think?"

"Maybe. I'm not a psychic, though."

She shouldered me gently and nodded to my mug. "I bet that chocolate is cool enough, now. Why don't you have a sip and I'll tell you my scary story first. You can go after me. We can make more when it's your turn."

I curled tighter and drank, pulled my beanie over my eyebrows. The story she told was about a butcher's daughter who became possessed by an evil spirit and began skinning her father's customers when they came to the shop after sundown.

"Eventually, the town came for her, so she fled to the woods with all her skinning knives," she said. She passed her hand through the air as if flaying a ribbon of flesh. "In the woods, the possession grew stronger, transforming her into a hideous witch who slept beneath the mud. Every full moon, she would wander into town, looking for sleeping children. She'd find them and skin them alive and bring their skin back to the woods where she'd stuff it with mud and branches and the child would come to life as a mud child, and the mud would pipe through the eye holes like playdough whenever it cried." She cupped her ear to the wind as if she could hear the mud children crying out there in the dark. "She'll hunt again this full moon. And the next. Over and over and so it goes." She always ended her stories with that line, as if every tale cycled back to the beginning, the madness of infinity adding to the terror.

The hair rose on the back of my neck.

Maisy's eyes sparkled with whatever light there was. Starlight, mostly. She could tell I'd gotten spooked and that I'd stopped worrying about Mama.

Then we heard that awful F-250 screaming around the bend.

Tires howling, headlights sweeping the treetops.

Lou's truck squealed into the driveway and all the doors opened and shut. I heard him scream and cuss, barking orders. I heard Mama's voice, too. And another man we knew only as Cowboy, a friend of Lou's we'd seen around the house over the past month or two.

I wanted to run inside, but Maisy grabbed me tight and held on.

A flashlight swept the yard. Lou and Cowboy appeared, carrying a long blanket with something heavy wrapped inside. Mama swung the flashlight erratically. Whenever the light caught Lou, I saw bloodstains on his shirt, blood up and down his arms.

"Keep the damn light on the ground, Carolyn," Lou shouted. "If I step in a gopher hole it'll be your ass."

"They're ground squirrels, Lou," said Cowboy. "They don't bury their holes like gophers do." Cowboy always talked fast and loud, like he'd had too much coffee.

"I don't give a red hot shit what they are. Hold up your end."

9

They sidestepped toward the creek, Mama close behind. The men swore and griped, the weight of their load hammocked between them. The light swung our way a couple times and I thought for sure they'd spot us. On the second pass of the flashlight, Cowboy misstepped and fell hard on his side, the contents of the blanket spilling over the ground.

A dead woman.

Blonde with green bangs.

Her arm twisted backward at the elbow, face bloody.

"Dammit, Carolyn," Lou growled. "I warned your skinny ass."

Mama sat in the dirt with the flashlight at her side, crying.

"I can't do this," she said. "I can't. I'm gonna go check on the kids."

"Like hell you are," said Lou. I could see that snarl from where we sat, even in the dark. It went halfway up his cheek. He had a shovel in his hand and he pointed it at her. "This was all your fault to begin with. Now hold the light like I told you."

Mama put her face in her hands and sobbed.

"Don't say that, Lou." She tried to catch her breath, the words coughing out in bursts. It took all I had from running to her and throwing my arms around her. I hated to see Mama cry. After a moment or two, she caught her breath and said: "It wasn't all my fault. You know how it happened."

Lou kicked the ground and a clod burst up, dirtying her face. "It happened 'cause you were diggin' in my goddamn pocket, looking for dope."

"You asked me to."

"I said wait till we hit the freeway."

"Don't put it all on me."

"Not gonna tell you again, Carolyn. *Shine the light.*"

Mama pointed the light down the hill.

Cowboy had the dead woman by the ankles, dragging her down to the creek. A pin-like bone jutted from her forearm and her head rolled on her shoulders like a dead bird. Mama got to her feet slowly. The light flickered and she tapped it in her palm and followed Cowboy down the grade. Lou hurried after them both.

As soon as we heard that shovel ticking at the dirt, we slipped around the Grandfather Tree and scurried up to the house through the backdoor. It still smelled like oatmeal inside. Our bowls sat on the table where we'd left them, chocolate powder spilled over the counter. We didn't even take our jackets off, just slipped into our beds with the covers up to our chins. I couldn't believe what I'd seen, like one of Maisy's stories had come to life. When I finally caught my breath, I heard the hiss of that distant shovel as it struck the ground. Sometimes five seconds between loads, sometimes ten. But the sound kept up like they were digging straight through to the other side of the planet.

I thought maybe the sound of that shovel was all I'd ever hear again.

3

WE WOKE TO THE SMELL of cupcakes.

The oven door groaned open and shut, open and shut. Utensils clattered and jangled in the steel sink.

We crept into the hallway, looking up and down for signs of Lou or Cowboy. Sometimes Cowboy slept on the couch and he'd scare us the way he'd stretch and yawn so loud, his gut inflating with those first morning breaths. But the living room was empty. The only sounds in the house came from the baking tins and cupboard doors. Mama came around the corner with a cutting board lined up with cupcakes, half vanilla and the rest chocolate. She'd done her hair and makeup already, that signature blue tint to her eyeliner and hair-sprayed curls bouncing over her forehead. Maybe she'd put herself together to show us it was a special occasion, that it meant something to her. Still, she looked exhausted underneath it all. Eyes red and swollen like she'd been crying the whole night through.

Maybe we all looked that way.

"I didn't forget, sweeties," she said. A little piece of chocolate hung at the corner of her mouth like she'd been tasting as she went. One of the perks of being the cook, she'd say. "You wouldn't believe it, but Lou hit a deer last night and put us straight into a ditch. We were stranded on the road for hours."

Of course we didn't believe it.

"Are you hurt?" Maisy said, looking her over.

"Just a couple of bumps. Lou got banged up a little. Bloodied his shirt."

"What about the deer?" I asked. I knew right away I shouldn't have said it. I only made the lie bigger by pressing on. I still didn't know exactly what happened, what horrors had brought it all about, but I was making her think of that dead woman instead of the make-believe deer.

We were all thinking about the dead woman.

Mama's eyes got wet and she gave a quick glance out the kitchen window toward the creek.

"I don't know Benny boy," she said. "I sure hope it's okay."

She set down the cutting board and handed out the cupcakes. Chocolate for me, vanilla for Maisy. They tasted just like heaven.

"They're delicious Mama," I said.

It was the praise she'd been waiting for. Big pearly smile.

"Still warm?"

"Yeah, still warm. How many can we have?"

"Today's a special day and you can have as many as you want." Mama held up a finger and found her handbag on the table. She took out a little white envelope. "I got another surprise for you little monsters."

She opened the envelope and flashed all-day passes to the Beach Boardwalk, the seaside amusement park just down the mountain in Santa Cruz. We'd gone once before when one of Mama's old flames paid our way, some older man with a wiry gray mustache and a one-syllable name. Nice enough guy, even though he couldn't take his hands off Mama. We never saw him again, but the soft serve ice cream, corn dogs, video arcades, and the blur and whirl of amusement park rides with their flashing lights and throngs of screaming kids—*that* stuck with us.

"A regular gave them to me," said Mama. "He said his grandkids never visit anymore and he didn't want the passes to go to waste. Well, don't you want to go?" She dangled the passes out of reach and we nearly tackled her to the ground to get them into our greedy hands. For the rest of the morning, all we talked about was junk food and fast rides. Mama looked us over proudly and complained how big we'd gotten and wondered where all the time had gone.

Three weeks went by and we began to worry if Mama would fulfill her promise to take us to the Boardwalk. We had run-ins with Lou almost every day, and his mood seemed to make every shadow in the house a little darker. We wondered how Mama even put up with it. He worked on his truck constantly and had all sorts of tools set up in the driveway. He'd removed the front bumper of the F-250, and used a big buzzsaw to break it down into smaller parts. Whenever he brought that saw down, it cast colorful sparks all over the front yard. Big ribbons of light that winked in the green grass. That's when I first caught a glimpse of the smashed-up bicycle. He carried it to the backyard and set it upside-down beside the tool shed, front wheel missing, handlebars twisted in on themselves. I watched him from the kitchen window as he cut it up piece by piece with a large hacksaw. When I saw him burying the pieces in the backyard, I asked Mama what he was doing and how strange I thought it was. She had trouble explaining it away, saying that grown men sometimes buried things and someday I might do the same.

I knew better. Had it happened a year ago, maybe I'd have gone along with whatever they wanted us to believe. But I'd grown just enough to make sense of it, to understand the stakes. A dead woman with green bangs lay buried in our backyard along with a demolished ten-speed and a dozen pieces of Lou Holt's front bumper. I'd seen her with my own eyes. Maisy too. We knew Lou killed that woman. He killed her and he buried the evidence, one bloody piece of chrome at a time, and I was old enough to understand why he needed to be so damn careful.

4

BY THE FOURTH OF JULY, we'd finally worn Mama down.

She hadn't been herself since that night by the creek. She often looked sick, the wisps of hair by her ears dark with sweat. She skipped meals, saying she *felt a little woozy*. Or *a little blah*. Other times she slept so hard we could barely wake her. We'd find her on the bed, curled beneath the open window, the room reeking of smoke and vinegar. She wouldn't move even when we shook her. Once we tried to get Lou to wake her but he told us to leave her alone, that dealing with us rotten kids made her exhausted. Maisy started calling it the *Lou flu*, since it got worse the more he hung around.

Still, we must have caught her on a good day. Lou was off on a long-haul job and Mama seemed anxious to leave the house for once. They'd cut her hours at the diner, so she'd been spending more time at home. Sometimes I'd catch her staring out the back windows at all the little holes Lou had dug. Like if she stared long enough, the grass would grow back and erase everything. It was here at the window, with that faraway look on her face, that we finally convinced her to drive us down the mountain.

We could hardly sit still in the car, thinking of all the

fun we'd have. Mama straightened the old Honda after a big hairpin turn. Large scrapes marred the redwood trees where cars had strayed too close to the edge. We were always glad to take that turn with Mama, rather than *Lou-the-speed-demon-maniac*. He'd tell us to clench our cheeks and he'd spin the wheel so hard the seatbelts would lock and we'd get bruises on our necks.

"Best to do all the rides before the ice cream," said Maisy. "Otherwise you'll puke your guts out."

"I wouldn't care if I puked," I said. "It would make more room for the corn dogs."

"That's gross."

"I'm just saying. Who knows when we'll go again?"

"No need to gorge yourselves," said Mama. "The world won't end tonight. We'll come back again by the end of the summer."

"You think you can get more passes?" I said.

"If it keeps you from stuffing your sweet little faces, then I'll talk to my regular and see what he can do for us. It's all about being as polite as you can, you know. You draw more flies with honey. You'd be wise to remember that."

"Lou isn't polite," said Maisy. "I guess you can draw flies with dog shit, too."

I laughed at that, but Mama took a harsh tone. "Don't talk trash about Lou, Maisy girl," she said. "He isn't here to defend himself. Besides, he'll come back with money to buy bread and oatmeal and hot chocolate. All the things you little monsters gobble up all day long. Maybe he's gruff because you haven't given him much of a chance."

Maisy had a reply for this too, but I grabbed her elbow and tipped my head in Mama's direction. We still weren't far from home. She could change her mind and turn right back around without a single word about it. Mama would often go out of her way to make a point.

"I'm sorry, Mama," said Maisy with her jaw tight and eyes squinting like the words hurt when they came out. She'd rather have done just about anything else in the world than give an apology. Anything but ruin our trip to the Boardwalk, that is.

"You'll be sorry when he leaves us," Mama said. I saw sweat beading at her temples again. Her face grew pale and the freckles around her eyes stood out. "We'll be eating kitchen scraps from the back of the diner if he does."

We didn't say a word the rest of the drive.

We reached Santa Cruz around four o'clock and pulled onto Beach Street, the sky clear and blue. The way the sunlight played on the water reminded me of all those sparks from Lou's buzzsaw. We saw the white scaffolding of the Giant Dipper, the park's biggest ride, and heard the growl of the ridecars as they torqued around the turns at breakneck speed. Everywhere I looked was a frenetic thrillride of colors and crowds and big improbable things.

Mama parked in the hourly lot and we tugged her the whole way to the ticket entrance. A teenage girl with a metallic smile tied our passes around our wrists and we hightailed down the walk, past popcorn carts and pretzel machines and girls in barely-there bikinis. Mama could hardly keep up. She called to us and stooped with her hands resting on her knees and then she'd hustle after us when she caught her breath. We ate soft serve ice cream with chocolate shells, our toes in the sand, gulls crowding us from every angle.

After a few rides, Mama called us in and told us she

had to find a bathroom and that she felt woozy again. Even though Lou was somewhere far away, that awful flu managed to get the better of her. She put a hand to her forehead and shuffled to the nearest bathroom and told us to wait outside and not wander off. With so much to see, we had trouble staying put. A sky tram trundled overhead with kids dangling their sandaled feet over the side, game prize animals in their laps. Teenagers on rollerblades circled through the crowd, stealing french fries from the unsuspecting. There was a carnival barker across the way trying to attract a crowd for the strong-man game. We watched as macho guys in muscle shirts took turns sending the puck as high as they could strike it, but never once ringing the bell.

Mama took forever in the bathroom.

"Maybe you should go check on her," I told Maisy.

She leaned into the doorway. "I don't see her. You think she fell asleep again?"

Women came and went, but Mama wasn't among them. Maisy wandered past the stalls, calling to her, but she still didn't respond. We took in the sights a while longer. The light in the sky had changed a little, but we still had an hour or two before dark. Rays of evening light spilled through the scene. We saw a kid on the sky tram drop his ice cream cone and watched it disinte-grate on the hot pavement. A gang of gulls swooped in, shrieking and biting.

I heard a commotion in the bathroom. A man's voice, barking orders. I never even saw him go in. Then came a loud crash and more reprimands. A security guard appeared in the doorway, holding Mama by the arm. She could barely put one foot in front of the other. In her hand she held a dirty square of tin foil like she'd just melted a piece of chocolate.

"Beat it, you goddamn junkie," he said. He let go and she folded to the ground. "Beat it or I'll call the police."

We ran to her, tried to help her up. Neither of us knew what was happening, only that the man growled when he spoke and he kept talking about the police. When he saw us helping Mama to her feet, he softened a little.

"This your mother?" he asked us.

We waited for Mama to respond for us, but she just fluttered her eyes. A crowd formed, everyone staring at us. Mama's tank top had fallen over her shoulder and one of her breasts hung halfway out. We didn't know what to do. We started crying at the same time. Big streaming tears. The security guard dropped his shoulders and knelt down, looked us hard in the eyes.

"You kids got someone you can call? I can take you to a phone."

We shook our heads. Maisy said, "No sir."

"No dad or grandparent?"

"No sir. Nobody."

"I think the police might help," he said. His name tag said Edwin. He had a dark, closely shaved goatee that looked as if it were drawn with a black marker. His lips drooped into a frown and his goatee drooped down with it.

"Can't you set us in a booth somewhere?" said Maisy, wiping her eyes with the back of her hand. "She'll get better in a bit. She just has the flu."

"The flu, huh?"

"That's right. It makes her really sleepy."

The security guard shooed the gawkers and turned and watched us with a sad look. He scooped the dirty tinfoil off the ground and rolled it in his palm until he had sculpted a cigar-shaped ornament. He kept looking at us. It felt like he wanted to tell us something but didn't know how to put it.

"Tell you what," he said, finally. "I feel a little sorry for you kids. There's a bench over there in the shade. Why don't we get your mom to rest up for a few minutes? I'll send the nurse over. Maybe she'll call an ambulance and maybe she won't. It's up to her. But I'll be honest with you kids, you're either leaving in an ambulance or in a squad car. It's one or the other. I can't let your Mom drive you nowhere in her condition."

Mama straightened her top and took a sideways step, then another. We helped her get to the bench and she sat with her face in her hands, Maisy and I perched on either side like gargoyles. The nurse never came. Mama dozed on and off for an hour or two and when she finally woke, the sun had set and she found herself in a dreamscape of neon banners and pulsing carousels and clown faces flashing bright electric teeth and the smell of sea air and warm concrete and cotton candy—and she quietly declared that it was time to go home.

5

SOMETHING ELSE HAPPENED that night at the Boardwalk that changed everything for us. Or maybe things had already changed and this one thing brought it all to a head. It happened as we walked through the parking lot, looking for our old Honda. In all our excitement to get our day passes we never checked our lot number, and we wandered forever through a labyrinth of hazy street-lights and paper trash and other Hondas that looked like ours. Slips of paper lay folded under all the wiper blades as if someone had come through advertising some local business. I had seen similar flyers before for car washes and sandwich shops.

But these weren't car wash coupons.

They were flyers for a missing woman.

Her name was Jessie Barton. She lived in Boulder Creek and disappeared on the tenth of June. The photo showed a happy blonde with bangs and different colored streaks in her hair. She sat on a patio with a tabby cat resting in the crook of her arm. Bold capital letters advertised a tip line and a fifteen-thousand-dollar reward.

Mama backed up with the notice still clipped to the

windshield, but before she cleared the parking lot, she stopped and had me get out and take it down. She didn't even know what it was, didn't seem to care much at all. Maisy and I read it together in the backseat, tracing every contour of the woman's face while Mama weaved through tourist traffic. Alice in Chains came on the radio and she growled the words to the song, slapping the downbeats on the steering wheel.

Maisy elbowed me and tapped the date above the photo, the date she went missing.

"The last day of school," she said. *"It's her."*

I took the flyer and offered a grim nod. I didn't know how to resolve the two images of Jessie Barton in my mind. The girl in the photograph looked like she'd spend the next sixty years petting cats and dying her hair all the colors of the rainbow, but the other—the one seared in my memory—would spend forever in a loop getting dragged by her ankles to her creekside grave. *Over and over and so it goes*, as Maisy would say.

When we pulled onto the highway, Maisy folded the paper and slipped it in her front pocket. At home, she tucked it into her homework binder where it stayed hidden for the next three weeks.

6

WHEN LOU CAME BACK from the road, he looked like he'd been fist fighting all across America—and losing every single fight he got himself into. His two bottom teeth were gone and a purple half-moon hung under his left eye. He limped around the house and he swore *goddammit* every time he got up from the chair. Nobody knew what happened and he wouldn't talk about it, not even to Mama. Sometimes he'd talk to himself, though. He'd stare out the back window smoking his pipe and soon he was nothing but mumbles and urgent questions asked to nobody but the empty room. The pipe he smoked didn't look anything like Sherlock Holmes, but a little glass pipe that he'd torch with a cheap gas station lighter and spit out white smoke like kettle steam.

Maisy and I stayed out of his way the best we could. We'd sit under the Grandfather tree and she'd play her harmonica and I'd read books and draw in the shade of that big old redwood. We hadn't gone down to the creek since that night in early June. Sometimes we'd get close, just close enough to see the patches of earth that had been dug up and refilled. They looked like little bald scabs on the hillside, still unclaimed by the wild grass.

24

At night we'd tell scary stories and Maisy would whisper a tale of ghostly revenge where Jessie Barton drifted up the hillside with her bloody face and green bangs and arms that bent crooked at the elbow and she'd coax poor Lou Holt out of bed in the way only ghosts can do. He'd follow her out the front door in a sleepwalk and head straight down the mountain road where some good ol' boy in a three-quarter-ton pickup would turn him into greasy roadkill. Each time she told the story, she'd add a new detail or a little extra dialogue so that it got longer and a little better each time.

But as good as the story got, Lou kept sucking wind. Sometimes we just couldn't avoid him.

One morning, just after daybreak, he came into our bedroom while we slept and dumped a glass of cold water on my face. I swam out of bed, gasping.

"Wake up, pussy nuts," he said.

"Why'd you do that?"

He curled a fist in the air. "Ask me why *one more time*."

I swept the wet hair out of my face, wiped the water from my eyes.

I couldn't tell if the look he gave was one of disgust or amusement.

"Put your clothes on," he said. "I've got a job for you."

A moment later, I found myself in the front seat of Lou's tow truck, chewing on a heel of white bread I'd snagged from the cupboard. A silver Cadillac hung from the tow cables in the back. It looked new, or close to new.

"Whose car is that?" I asked, through a mouthful of bread.

"It don't matter whose car it is," he said.

"Then where are we taking it?"

"You're going to help me strip it for parts."

I didn't know what that meant. The whole thing made me very nervous. If Lou wanted me to work for him, he'd soon be watching me closely. If I did a bad job, maybe he'd try to punish me for it. He'd never hurt me before, but with Mama sick, there wasn't anyone to stick up for me if he did. Nobody but Maisy, that is.

Lou gunned the tow truck up the mountain. The left-over night mist dissolved over the road, blue sky marbled in the white. The way he drove, I wondered how he even kept the truck on the blacktop. I clutched the seatbelt strap with both hands as if I dangled over a bottomless pit. Every now and then, he'd look me over and snicker to himself, judging me with those icy blue eyes.

He wheeled onto a rock road near the summit, the sound of loose dirt and stones grinding beneath us as we went. We passed through brambles of tanoaks and coyote brush, and soon the road dipped and turned into a wide meadow littered with the husks of many cars. A black dog barked as we drew near, pacing back and forth on a chain. A skinny blond man with sores on his face came up to the driver window and spoke to Lou about the Cadillac.

"This here's John MacLeod," said Lou. "He pretty much runs this place. You do what he says while I take care of some business in the trailer." He nodded toward the back of the meadow where a few run-down RVs sat under the oak trees.

"Tiny hands," said MacLeod, flicking a finger at me. "Good call, Lou."

MacLeod told me to call him Mac and said that he'd been *kneecapped* not too long ago and couldn't get down low, and that the thing he hated most was removing the seats from the cars people brought him. He gave me a silver ratchet and plugged a socket at the end of it and told me where to find the bolts. It didn't take long to get the hang of it. In a few minutes, I had the first two bolts loose in my hands. The seat wobbled in its tracks, and I climbed into the car to work on the final two bolts. Before long, I'd wrestled the whole seat out of the Cadillac and had it resting in the dirt.

"Not bad, kid," said MacLeod. "I'll talk to Lou. I see a career opportunity here." He smiled and it took me by surprise. Rotten teeth like wooden pegs, gums bleeding. I'd never seen an uglier face in my life. He itched at a sore on his forehead and returned to his work.

I looked around for Lou, but I couldn't spot him. The temperature had risen inside the Cadillac and sweat darkened the collar of my shirt. It was plenty warm outside the car, too. The junkyard was heating up with the smell of redwood needles and dirty engine grease. Heat haze shimmered over a field of dry rattlesnake grass. If Lou wanted to dump a cold glass of water on my face, I'd have surely let him.

"What's he doing in that trailer?" I asked.

MacLeod snickered. "He's paying a visit to Sharla Ray."

"Who's that?" I thought the name sounded like a movie star.

"You'll find out soon enough, little buddy. See, I work the chop shop and Sharla Ray works the trailer. It's what you call cross-marketing."

Another car drove up and a man and woman got out. They didn't look much better than MacLeod, like they'd been lost in the forest for weeks and just found their way out. I started working on the passenger seat, but the new arrivals took notice of me. They came around to my side of the car, laughing.

"Who's this, Mac?" said the man, scratching at his stringy gray hair. One ear hung sadly lower than the other like he'd lost it in an accident and they couldn't sew back on straight enough. I imagined him getting teased plenty about it and tried not to look. "You got little kids boosting cars for you now?"

"He ain't boosting cars, Kenny," said Macleod. "Just helping with the grunt work. Lou brought him."

Kenny eyed the tow truck and scanned the field. He pulled at his sad ear and wiped a sheen of sweat from his forehead. "Lou's here?"

"That's his truck ain't it?"

Kenny exchanged glances with the woman, then returned his attention to me.

"Well, damn kid," said Kenny. "That looks like a tough job—a real *ball-buster.*"

"It's not too bad," I said.

"Whenever I got a tough job, you know what I do?"

"What?"

He gave me the creeps and I wished he wouldn't talk to me. I looked around for Lou, but he still hadn't come out of the trailer. Whatever he and Sharla Ray were up to seemed to be taking a long time. I figured maybe she was a psychic and giving him some kind of palm reading.

"Well, I'll tell you what I do. I take a big hit of crystal and it does the work for me. Like a turbo boost. Next thing you know, the work's all done and you're on to the next damn thing."

"Come on, Kenny," said the woman. "Don't tease him."

"I ain't teasing him," Kenny said. He unpocketed a glass pipe with a charred bulb at the end like the kind Lou smoked. "Wanna give it a shot, superboy?"

"No," I said, flatly. I tried to ignore him, but he just

wouldn't quit. He crouched beside me and fed the pipe with little glassy shards from a mini ziplock bag. Then he wagged a cigarette lighter underneath. It crackled. White smoke bloomed from the hole in the pipe. He took a noisy drag like it burned his throat and blew the smoke in my face.

I wheeled back and coughed. I recognized the smell from when Lou smoked in the kitchen. A weird, vaguely chemical smell like hot plastic.

"Stop it, Kenny," said the girl. "You're going to get him high."

"That's the point, sugar," he said. He broke out in a crazy laughing jag. That sad little ear drooping with each breath. "Aw man, no nap-time for this kiddie today."

"That's enough," said MacLeod.

"I'm just having fun, Mac." He took another hit and cornered me against the Cadillac, cheeks big and swollen. He seemed to be having a damn good time with it. I held my breath, expecting another toxic plume, but the smoke never came. I don't know how Lou crossed the field so quickly, especially since his limp hadn't quite straightened out yet, but he now had a fistful of Kenny's hair wound up in his hand, yanking him backward. One hard punch to the kidney and Kenny crumpled to the dirt.

Lou didn't stop. He kicked him in the gut six or seven times.

Blow after merciless blow.

The woman screamed at Lou, and MacLeod inched between them.

"All right, Lou," said MacLeod. "One more and you're liable to kill him."

"Nobody would miss him," said Lou, breathing hard.

He stood hunched, with his hands on his knees, sweating. "Ain't the first time this sonofabitch stirred shit up, Mac. Ain't the first goddamn time." He bunched Kenny's shirt, hoisted him a few inches off the ground and landed another blow square to the eye.

I didn't know what to do. I'd never seen an ass-kicking like that before. A few schoolyard scuffles, maybe. But nothing close to that. My hand curled so tight over the ratchet that it visibly shook.

Lou looked me up and down.

"You can't let people corner you like that," he said.

"What was I supposed to do?" I clenched my teeth, stared at the ground, trying everything to keep from crying. I knew it would only make Lou angry.

"Go ahead and give him a kick."

I shook my head. "I'm not going to kick him."

The girl kept shouting. Lou wagged his fist and she shut up real quick.

"Just once," said Lou. "I'm teachin' you a lesson, here. Do it."

I stood over Kenny. He lay curled like a baby, gray hair sprawled all around him. Blood draining from his mouth. Groaning.

He looked half-dead or worse.

"Do it, goddamnit. Or I swear to God I will—"

I hauled back and kicked Kenny in the mouth.

He grunted and buried his face in his hands.

Lou didn't think I'd do it. He looked stunned. Then he jutted his lip and gave a proud nod.

"That's it," said Lou. "Now tell him to fuck off."

I shook my head. I couldn't hide the tears now.

"Say *fuck off, Kenny.*"

I glanced at Lou, glanced at the bloodied man before me.

"Fuck off, Kenny," I said.

"Louder."

"FUCK OFF, KENNY," I screamed. It came out wild and raw, like it had been sitting there building pressure. Something coiled tight and spring-loaded. Like I'd been waiting my whole life to scream those words at some bloody, ass-kicked bastard. It felt so good that I screamed it again.

And again.

"That's more like it."

We left a few minutes later. Lou and I didn't talk the whole way. He didn't even drive too crazy down the mountain. We passed our house and he kept driving the few extra miles into town, straight into the parking lot of a Foster's Freeze. Lou ordered a double cheeseburger and fries with a coke and I ordered a cheeseburger and a chocolate shake. We didn't speak a word. Lou flicked on the radio and we listened to Willie Nelson croon "Blue Eyes Crying in the Rain" while we ate and drank noisily, and when we finally sped back up the mountain and pulled up to the house, he unfolded a wad of cash from his shirt pocket and handed me a twenty-dollar bill. I took it and stuffed it deep into my jeans pocket.

Later that afternoon, Maisy found me sitting on my bed, staring at the money Lou'd given me. Watching him flip his lid had frightened me, but what I'd done scared me even more. I'd never felt that kind of rage in my life. I wondered if someday soon I'd be shit-kicking grown men within an inch of their lives and celebrating down at the Foster's Freeze with a burger and a tasty coke afterwards. I wondered if I'd become just like Lou.

"Are you hurt?" she asked, hovering over me.

"No, why?"

Maisy pointed to the tip of my shoe, caked with blood. She sat beside me and put her arm around my shoulders. "You ever feel like everything is just spinning out of control, brother? Like we're racing downhill with no brakes, just screaming away in the backseat and there's nothing we can do to stop it?"

I gave her a hard look. "Every damn day, sis."

7

NATURE HAS ITS OWN WAY of taking care of things. That's what Mama told us when a fawn got tangled up in the rotten fencing at the far end of the property. Maisy heard it first and woke me. Soon, Mama came out too, pinning her earrings and straightening her light blue work dress, running late as always. The three of us just stood there before this pitiful thing. It cried with the voice of a child calling *wah*, over and over without end.

"Oh Mama, can't we help her?" said Maisy. She looked even skinnier than usual under those behemoth redwoods with her ragged sweatpants and too-big flower shirt falling around her shoulders like a poor orphan girl. "She'll die if we don't do something."

Mama took her gently by the arms. "You leave that baby deer alone. The way it's crying, her mother's likely near and she's just waiting for us to leave. It'll work out just the way it's supposed to."

She shrunk out of Mama's hands. "Can I bring her a bowl of water?"

Mama flicked her eyes from the fawn to the brightening sky as if judging how late she'd be. I thought she looked skinny, too. Cheeks drawn in, shadowy bones beneath the eyes. Maybe her blond hair looked a little dirty blond now. I'd caught her inspecting herself in the long mirror more than once over the past month or so, pinching the waist of her work dress, tracing those sharp cheekbones with her fingertips. Like she'd been borrowing some part of herself and she'd been forced to give it back in a hurry.

"I have to go now, girly," she said. "Fetch some water if you want to, but don't you touch her. Not one bit."

I didn't understand why we couldn't pull that rickety fencing away and give the thing a chance. Neither did Maisy. When Mama finally left, we watched that poor animal from the kitchen window, bleating sadly to the empty yard, so utterly alone. It didn't drink the water we'd set out, didn't even notice it in the little pink cereal bowl.

After a while, I couldn't stand the sound anymore, or maybe that Maisy wouldn't stop obsessively watching from the window. I brought my sketchbook out to the road where I'd seen a patch of wild irises spring up and I sat cross-legged in the dying mid-summer grass, sketching out those dusky-purple petals with golden tongues, dark veins throughout. The heat came early that day. The sun felt heavy on my neck. When my legs went to sleep, I got up and teetered into the house for a glass of tap water. Maisy was no longer at the window. I drank the water and poured a second glass, looked around the house, calling for her. When I looked outside, there she was, yanking at the fencing and trying to free the baby deer. She saw me over her shoulder and motioned with her head.

"You gonna stand there or are you gonna help?" she called.

"Mama said to leave it—"

"Well she's not here, is she?" Her voice had an edge to it, like her tongue had grown sharp at the tip. "Lou isn't here either, is he?"

"No, thank goodness."

"So, I'm in charge now." Her eyes heated up. "I say you need to help me."

I couldn't help but chuckle at how forcefully she took charge, like our eleven-month difference turned into twenty years all of a sudden. I regretted laughing, though. She gave me a hard look when I did. It clearly mattered to her. I hadn't seen her so focused in all my life.

"I'll help you, Maze," I said.

The fawn suffered far worse injuries than we'd thought. Her hind leg folded outward at a gruesome angle, a pink-gray bone jutting through the copper fur. But the fencing had also torn the tender hide on the underside of her belly and a little red bubble welled from the wound. It didn't look right, like maybe her guts were getting ready to spill out. *Wah, wah, wah*, it bleated. Maisy held it by the scruff and I kicked and pulled at the rotting wood and rusty nails until I'd cleared enough to pull her free. She hooked her fingers under the haunches and I lifted from the shoulders and soon we'd hoisted her in the air, the little thing, and brought her to the back porch. She rested there on her side in the shade of the house, pink cereal bowl beside her, tongue lolled onto the wooden boards, panting silently.

"We need to bring her inside," said Maisy.

"Why?"

"So I can take care of her better." She had a certain manic seriousness to her now, hands trembling. I thought maybe her bones would rattle right out of her skin. "I can save her."

I eyed the creature.

That ruined leg. That ghastly wound.

"Maze," I started, but she wouldn't hear it.

"I'll do it myself if you don't help. Just to the kitchen is all."

I didn't like any of this. Part of me hoped the thing would die so the whole episode would be over before Mama got home. Certainly before Lou came home, whenever that would be. I felt so anxious I could feel blood chugging in my ears. Still, I couldn't say no to Maisy. She'd do anything I asked of her and we both knew it. But even though we had that kind of understanding, I didn't have to like it.

When we brought the fawn inside, I took another look at it, shook my head, and slipped into the bedroom. I lay curled on the bed, watching the redwood boughs through the window, how they swayed in the bright blue sky. My mind wandered. I thought of the hazel-eyed kid in my fourth-grade class named Stanley Robertson who never made it back from winter break. A car accident in Colorado, the teacher had said. The other kids gossiped that the Robertsons went over a cliff in their Ford Aerostar and it wiped out the whole family. I thought about their bones breaking through their skin just like the deer, just like Jessie Barton. All torn up with pink guts popping through the wounds. I didn't want to live in a world where bones and guts popped out of anything. Not baby deer, not women on ten-speeds, not hazel-eyed boys named Stanley. I suddenly felt the world was an impossibly cruel and violent place.

Lou's truck roared into the driveway.

I sat up, pressed my face to the window. Cowboy popped out of the passenger side first, rambling on a mile a minute. Lou was telling him he was a dumbshit, but chuckling all the while. They seemed too happy, stumbling over the driveway and laughing. Drunk, maybe. Each carried a six pack of Old Milwaukee under their arms, hooting and cussing at each other good-naturedly. Lou chuckled through the song *Oh Lord, Won't You Buy Me a Mercedes Benz* as he went through the front door.

I ran down the hall to warn Maisy, knowing it was too late.

She probably heard them coming anyway. The whole world did.

"Goddamn," said Cowboy. He was the first to find Maisy sitting on the kitchen floor, the fawn crudely bandaged with linens from the hall cupboard. "Looks like your girl found a new pet."

I couldn't read Lou's expression at first, like one of those game show wheels spun in his head, little pegs ticking away all the possible reactions. It finally landed on a type of amused disbelief.

"Girl, it ain't even huntin' season yet," said Lou, with a chuckle. "Even if it was, you wouldn't find much meat on that sucker."

She didn't react, just rocked the creature in her arms. It might have been dead by now, glassy eyes like drops of molasses, pink tongue hanging sadly from its mouth.

"Looks like it's bleedin'," said Cowboy. "What'd you shoot it with?"

"I didn't shoot it," she said.

"I never ate me a baby deer," said Lou. "Wonder if it tastes like veal?"

"Probably pretty close," said Cowboy.

"What do you think, Cowboy? Got any gut-hooks on you?"

"Shit," he said. "I can butcher a deer with any kind of blade. Up in Idaho I cleaned more'n I could count, all with my granddad's buck knife. Just a little three-incher."

"I don't want to hear about your little three-incher, sweetheart." Lou cracked a beer and took a big chug, wiped his mouth with his forearm. "Let's see what's under them bandages." He reached for the fawn and Maisy slapped the back of his hand. Hard, too. Lou pulled back, surprised. He might have slapped her in revenge if Cowboy hadn't burst into maniacal laughter.

"Look who's boss," said Cowboy, barely getting the words out. He swept the trucker hat off his head and screwed up his thick brown hair, belly rolling with each big laugh. His T-shirt read *Liquor in the Front, Poker in the Rear* and it rode a few inches above his hairy navel. "That's the first time I seen you lose a fight, Lou!"

Lou's face darkened, that tell-tale sneer crawling up his cheek. He reached for the fawn again and this time she punched him square in the gut. Cowboy howled, but Lou didn't think it was funny anymore.

"Here's the thing, girly," said Lou. "An animal like this, well somebody needs to put it down. It's what you're supposed to do. You know what that means?"

"I won't let you."

"You got no choice."

Lou set down the beer and palmed Maisy's forehead so she couldn't reach him, and with the other hand he grabbed the animal by the hind legs and lifted it into the air. The bandages fell away and it hung limp from his clenched fist, as if it had broken in every single place a creature could break. Maisy screamed as Lou marched into the backyard and set the animal down by the treeline—down where they'd buried the dead girl. He looked it over and spat in the grass.

"Girl, you been cradlin' a corpse," he said. "This thing's already a goner."

She collapsed in the dirt, sobbing into her hands. I came up behind her and put my arms around her, but she shrugged me away. I thought Lou would have thrown a fit about her getting physical with him, but he only seemed to pity her instead. He got another eyeful of the dead fawn, sucked his teeth, and headed back up the grade.

I couldn't get her to come back inside. She sat in the backyard until dark, tearing fistfuls of dead grass and throwing them up in the air. Moaning and wailing, pounding at the dirt. She came to bed late, just before Mama got home from her shift. Lou and Cowboy had settled down by then. By the sounds of it they were watching some action movie and drinking the last of the Old Milwaukee. I told her I was sorry, but she didn't say a thing to me.

In the morning, she got out of bed at first light and went scampering down the hall. She returned a few minutes later and slipped under the covers with the bedsheet pulled to her chin, shivering.

"She's gone," she said, staring at the ceiling.

"Gone?"

"Just disappeared."

"Maybe her mother came back for her."

"Yeah, maybe she did."

Lou asked later if I'd heard the coyotes yipping and howling all night long and I said I didn't hear a thing, even though it was a lie. I knew Mama had been right, that nature had its own way of taking care of things. I knew I lived in a world where innocent things lived and suffered and died, even though I wished it wasn't so. Maisy knew it too, though she fought it with everything she had.

8

OTHER THAN COWBOY, we never saw anyone come calling for Lou until the red-haired man showed up. It was just around sunset, maybe eight o'clock. There wasn't much light left on the road, just whatever was filtering low through the tanoak trees. Enough to see the red-haired man pacing back and forth on the driveway smoking cigarettes behind a beat-up, rust-colored Chevy Camaro. Crows gathered in the redwoods by the dozens and some of them were landing on the roof, pecking at the gutters and cawing like mad. They always seemed to wait for the rest to arrive before they went on their way. Like we were just some halfway point to someplace else. Someplace better, no doubt. It was the crows that got Maisy to look out the window. She spotted the man and we both watched him hiking up and down the driveway in a loop until he worked up the nerve to ring the doorbell.

Mama was working the swing shift and wouldn't be home until late. That left Lou in charge, but we hadn't seen him in a few hours and he wasn't answering the door.

The second ring went unanswered, too.

On the third ring, I nudged Maisy and she called to the man through the window screen. He shuffled over with his hands tucked tight under his armpits as if they were keeping him from floating away.

"Is Lou here?" he asked. He wore a constellation of freckles and there was a fresh scar that ran from his bottom lip clear under his chin. "I need to talk to him."

"He's probably drunk in the backyard and doesn't want to be bothered," said Maisy.

"Could you get him anyway?" There was a slight quake to his voice as if he were on the verge of losing his temper. Maybe he was just nervous. "He'll wanna see what I got to show him."

"We don't know where he is," I said, over Maisy's shoulder.

The man eyed me like some half-crazy dog, trying to get a look at my face through the screen. "Well, I ain't leaving till I talk to him," he said. He lit another cigarette and blew the smoke through the screen. "You don't want me to stand here and bug you kids all night long, do you?"

Maisy closed the window and pulled the blinds. "Rude," she said.

The man pounded on the window.

She took out her harmonica, tapped it on her palm and played.

He pounded again.

We could hear him saying: "I ain't leavin'."

Maisy gave a defeated look. "Should we find Lou?" she said.

"I don't think he's leaving, sis."

"Well, let's go looking for him, then."

We searched the house from one end to the other.

Just as we looked into the backyard, a flood light came on. Lou was standing by the tool shed and he had a ratty denim tarp rolled out with parts of an old rifle laid out around him. He was squatting over it and scratching his stubbly neck as if he'd forgotten how to put it all back together. He looked startled when Maisy opened the sliding door and called to him.

"What do you want?" he barked.

"There's a man here to see you."

"Tell him I ain't here, dammit."

"He says he won't leave till you talk to him."

"He ain't a cop?"

"I would have said he was a cop if he was a cop."

"Don't sass me. What's he look like?"

"Red-haired man with a scar on his chin. Smokes like a chimney and he's real jumpy."

Lou's face went blank for a moment, then something seemed to click. He rose and went around the side yard toward the front of the house and disappeared. We went back to our room, opened the blinds, and listened from the window. The porch light had come on, and we could see them at the extent of the light's reach. They were standing behind the Camaro and the red-haired man was telling him some kind of dramatic story and Lou was telling him to keep it down. I couldn't hear much of what was said after that, but when the trunk popped open, Lou seemed to get real interested in what he saw there.

After a while, we lost interest. We played blackjack on the floor with Jolly Rancher bets. It was something Lou taught us how to do before he started ignoring us for good. We'd take turns being the dealer every three hands.

"What do you think is in the trunk?" asked Maisy.

She was the dealer this time and probably trying to distract me so I'd make a mistake.

"Maybe some guy tied up with a handkerchief shoved in his mouth," I said.

"You watch too much TV."

"Maybe it's full of diamonds."

"A trunkful of diamonds? Get real."

"What do you think it is, Maze?"

She hit me with the ten of hearts. Busted.

"I think there's a boy inside that trunk who owes me another Jolly Rancher and he's just so sad about it he wants to cry. *Oh wait, that's you.*"

I flicked a candy at her and it bounced off her shoulder.

We played a few more hands and then we heard a truck pull into the driveway.

"Sounds like Cowboy's truck," said Maisy.

An intense conversation erupted. Cowboy, Lou, and the red-haired man all gabbing in harsh whispers and cuss words. We tried to ignore it, but the rantings had a conspiratorial nature and it kept drawing us in. Cowboy's truck fired up, and the Camaro engine revved. We couldn't ignore it anymore, so we turned out the bedroom lights and peeked through the window. It was dark now. Taillights glowing red. The truck and car had traded places, and the red-haired man was now backing the Camaro into the garage.

For a moment, all was quiet.

Then the bickering picked up again. We could hear Lou saying *ease up, ease up,* and Cowboy saying *bring it, bring it.* Something heavy hit the ground and we felt it shudder the walls of the house. Maisy and I gave each other a blank look. The men quarreled and cussed and soon their voices spilled into the backyard.

We snuck out to the kitchen and sat on either end of the sink, peering out the small window into the backyard. The flood light came on again, and we both shrunk away from the sudden light. When our eyes adjusted, we saw Lou, Cowboy, and the red-haired man all standing around a large safe with the spin dial pointing at the sky.

"I knew it was diamonds," I said.

"You don't know what's in there."

"They mostly keep diamonds in safes, Maze."

"Since when are you an expert on safes?"

"I just got a feeling about it."

"I guess we'll never know," she said, sadly.

"Why do you say that?"

"You think these dummies can figure out how to break into that big ol' thing? Looks like it's made out of Kryptonite."

I stole another glance out the window. The three men stood pointing at the safe, making general comments as if each had come from a long line of safecrackers. They'd take long pulls from their cigarettes, scratch their heads, spit, and point some more. They might as well have been looking at a flying saucer.

"Lou's a tow truck driver," I said. "He's got the right tools."

She gave me a wink and tapped both sides of her head. "Sure, but he's missing the most important tool of them all."

We both laughed.

I poured myself a bowl of cereal for dinner and went into the living room and flicked on the TV. Maisy wandered back to our room and I heard her flop on the bed. She turned on the radio and played along with her harmonica, switching from station to station to find a song in the right key. I shoveled a few mouthfuls of Rice Krispies and cycled through the Olympics, the nightly news, and some cop show rerun from the 1970s. I watched the cop show for a minute or two. Muscle cars were chasing each other through busy downtown streets, decimating newspaper stands and hot dog carts. The bad guys drove with blown-out glass, swerving all over the road. One guy took a bullet to the shoulder and drove off like no big deal, but it seemed to me getting shot in the shoulder would hurt just as bad as anywhere else.

I hadn't noticed the red-haired man wander in and pour himself a glass of water from the tap. He was leaning against the wall with sweat running down his face when he spoke to me.

"You like the X-Men, huh?" he said.

I looked down at my shirt—a worn-out image of Wolverine with his claws out. I'd dribbled some milk on it and I wiped it with my knuckles.

"Yeah, I guess so," I said.

"I've got a boy just about your age," he said. He gave a grin that didn't seem to have any meanness at all. Just the bare-naked grin and nothing else. "He lives down in Arizona. Man, he loves the X-Men. Gonna send him a bunch of shirts just like yours when I get some money."

Friendly as he seemed, I didn't know why he was telling me this.

"Cool," I said.

The sliding door opened and Lou stuck his head in.

"Hey, pussy nuts."

I gave him a long look and didn't respond.

"You know I'm talkin' to you, little shit." Lou was

trying to impress the red-haired man by bossing me around. "Come out here and earn your keep for once."

I set the bowl on the coffee table and scratched at a dark blemish in the wood. There were fresh scuff marks in the varnish where'd he'd flipped it against the wall heater a few weeks back. The wall heater had a few scuffs and dents of its own.

"Don't make me come in there and get your ass," said Lou.

I rose and shuffled to the sliding door, looked outside. They'd dragged the safe farther down the hill and set up the flood light with a long orange extension cord. Lou urged me onward until I stood looking over the safe. All I needed was a cigarette and I'd fit right in.

"Take this and tell me what you see," said Lou, handing me a small flashlight.

I clicked it on and pasted the safe with it.

"It looks like a safe, Lou."

Cowboy and the red-haired man laughed.

"Look inside, dummy," said Lou.

They'd managed to pry a corner of the door so it folded slightly open like a dog-eared page of a book. Just the smallest of openings. I shined the light and peered through the crack. Stacks of long yellow envelopes lay inside, encased in some kind of netting. It wasn't something you'd expect to see in a TV cop show. Too plain and boring. But there was a certain mystery to it. A mystery inside of a mystery. I stared into the hole until Lou grew impatient.

"Well?"

"Looks like a bunch of envelopes."

"We think there's money in those envelopes. What else do you see?"

I looked again and saw a couple dark objects among all the manilla paper like long toilet paper rolls. "There's something else but I don't know what it is."

"Long round sticks?"

"Yeah. Long round sticks. Two of them at least."

"They're big firecrackers," said Lou. "Don't get all worried about it. We just need you to reach in there and pull one of them out. They fell inside and didn't explode like we wanted."

"Explode?"

"They're firecrackers, just like I told you. But big ones."

They were hiding something from me. I didn't know what, but I sensed this whole ordeal was important to Lou and he was playing me someway.

"What'll you give me if I pull one of those things out?"

"Give you?" Lou heated up, his blue eyes smoldering in the flood lamp's shine. "What if I put my foot in your ass?"

"Relax, Lou," said Cowboy. "He's trying to help us."

"He can't even help himself."

"Were you guys trying to blow this thing open?" I asked. I must have sounded dumb when I said it. Of course they were trying to blow it open.

"Cowboy tried, but they fell in and nothing happened," said Lou.

"They're old," said Cowboy. "Found them in my uncle's shed. Maybe they don't even work no more. Could be duds."

"A hundred dollars," I said. It sounded like a good number.

Lou and Cowboy looked at each other.

"Fine," said Lou. "A hundred for a firecracker stick. I'll even give you another fifty if you light it for us."

I nodded and shook Lou's hand. "Deal."

I took one last look and fit my hand into the opening. Once I cleared my knuckles, my arm slipped in easily, then it got tighter the farther down I reached. My fingertips graced the rough paper jackets of the manilla envelopes. The nylon netting holding them all together. I felt the cool brass hardware. I was thinking of all the things I could buy with a hundred and fifty dollars when I found one of the waxy cardboard tubes and slowly worked it into my grasp.

"I think I've got it," I said.

"Good," said Lou. He'd taken a couple steps backwards. "Whatever you do, don't drop it."

"Why not?"

"Just don't."

I was up to my shoulder now, the jagged metal poking my skin. The thing was heavier than I thought, and it nearly slipped out of my hand as I brought it close to the opening. In order to pull it out, I had to dangle it lengthwise and extract it like a Jenga brick. I looked up at the three men and they'd taken yet another step back.

"What now?" I said casually, with the stick in my hand. By now, I knew what it was. I'd seen plenty of dynamite on TV. It felt cold and dead in my hands, like a paperweight. I couldn't imagine a thing like that going off without a spark. It seemed safe enough. But they were crazy if they thought I was going to go near it with an open flame. The wick had burned down near the blasting cap, curled and black and charred. I wouldn't light it for fifty dollars. Not even for a million.

Cowboy carefully took it out of my hands and nestled

it into the crude opening. He did it all at arm's length as if the extra few inches would help somehow. While he was situating the dynamite, Lou grabbed my wrist and slapped a bic lighter in my hands and asked if I knew how to use it.

"I changed my mind," I said, handing it back.

Lou wouldn't take it.

"We made a deal. You have to do this."

I dropped the lighter on the ground and started to walk away, but he grabbed my wrist again.

"Let go, Lou."

"That money inside will keep this place up for years," he said. He said it in a stupid, pleading voice that sounded about as sincere as a local mattress commercial. "New roof, fresh paint. Don't you want to give your mama some peace of mind, son?"

I glanced at the safe, the dynamite placed just so. That sooty wick curling from the tip like a bird's claw. I didn't trust Lou one bit. But I thought about Mama and how maybe she'd get better with all that money. How she wouldn't have to worry about keeping up the house as much. Maybe she could quit her job and find something better.

"I'll do it," said the red-haired man. He walked up and plucked the lighter out of the dirt, gave it a few flicks. "All that stress might activate your claws, Wolverine."

I nodded gratefully and backed away—all the way to the Grandfather tree.

The red-haired man sat beside the safe and studied the dynamite very intently as if there were some complicated puzzle to be solved. He flicked the lighter a few times from a safe distance while he contemplated. Then he got himself into a runner's position like I'd seen in the Olympics, reaching back with one hand near the wick and the other planted in the dirt. He rocked back and forth, testing his legs. He glanced over at Lou and Cowboy, who had both drifted further down the hill.

I heard the zip and click of the sparkwheel.

Once, twice.

On the third flick, the red-haired man jumped up and bolted down the hill. He'd only taken three or four steps when the backyard filled with an intense yellow light. The blast followed, a double-boom that was the loudest damn thing I'd ever heard. It knocked me flat on my butt, twigs and dirt and other debris raining down all around me. Maisy came running out from the back of the house, looking me over in a panic.

"You okay?" she said. "What happened?"

I got to my feet, checked my face for blood. The air smelled strange and there was a funny taste in my mouth.

"Dynamite," I said.

We both looked down the hill.

Lou and Cowboy were coming up slowly while the red-haired man lay face-down in the grass. The flood light had completely disappeared, and they were training their flashlights on the red-haired man. He wasn't moving. Bits of paper fluttered all around like confetti. The sky was filled with it. Lou went to the safe and looked it over. The door was off. He stared at it a moment, then shined the light into the sky at all the strange paper snow. You could see birds up there scattering in every direction, interrupting the starlight. He kneeled over the safe and pulled out a torn manilla envelope.

"What is it?" said Cowboy. "What's inside?"

Lou tore off what remained of the blistered yellow paper.

"Titty magazines," he said.

"Titty magazines?"

Lou held one up and showed him.

"Well, what else is there? Can't be all there is."

Lou didn't have an answer.

They searched the ground with their flashlights, searched the trees. They looked like a pair of explorers lost in the deep woods. Lou held out his hand and captured a few motes of paper still drifting down from the treetops. His face held a child's sense of wonder.

The red-haired man groaned. They wandered over and helped him sit up. He looked about with wild, glassy eyes. His shirt had torn clean off and there was blood leaking from his nose and mouth, red hair standing on end like a comic book character.

"You know where he lives?" asked Lou.

"Yeah, I know where he lives," said Cowboy.

"Can you take him home?"

"Yeah. What about the money?"

"You blind? Ain't no fuckin' money. Just titty magazines."

Cowboy took off his hat and inspected the brim, shook it against his leg.

"Goddamn," he said.

"Goddamn is right," said Lou.

The red-haired man began to cry.

I BEGAN TO WAKE in the early hours, when the fog sat low and thick in the trees and made everything look like a dream. I'd sit alone at the dining table and stare out through the glass door at the cottony pre-dawn, wondering if all the people of the world had suddenly vanished, if somehow I was chosen to watch the world empty out and grow cold. These were lonely times, but peaceful ones, too. Just the eerie drift of fog and coyotes yip-howling in the dark. Then, just as the sky began to change, I'd tiptoe down the hall and quietly slip into bed as if I'd just gotten away with something. Maybe it was the first thing I learned to steal—not cash or jewelry or stupid gadgets—but moments. Quiet, peaceful moments.

One morning, before I'd snuck back into bed, I heard the floor creak and I looked up to see a silhouette standing at the mouth of the hall. My stomach felt weightless for a moment as I worried who it might be. I straightened, felt my eyes strain to make it out. Then, Mama's soft voice came low and hushed from the shadows.

"That you, Benny?"

She said it like she knew it was me, but didn't know what else to say.

"Yeah," I whispered. "Just getting a glass of water."

"I don't see any water."

"I was about to."

She went to the cupboard and found a plastic cup, filled it from the tap. She set it in front of me and rested her fingertips atop my head and gave my scalp a quick scratch. It annoyed me when she did that before school, since I had to fix my hair in the car's side mirror without looking like I cared at all. But on an early summer morning with just the two of us, I didn't mind. It reminded me of the way things were before Lou showed up.

She turned and went to the living room, and for a moment I thought she was going back to bed without another word. Instead, she pulled the old afghan blanket off the couch, the one hiding the dark brown stain from some long-ago spill, and she came and sat next to me at the dining table. She sat close and shalled the blanket around us both, like we were two bugs in a cocoon. I rested my head on her shoulder and she raked her fingernails over my scalp until I nearly fell asleep.

"You know, your father used to sit in the dark," she said. I blinked myself awake. She didn't talk about him much, so when she did, I listened. "He had a long commute over the mountain, so he'd wake up early and eat breakfast before sunrise. I'd find him drinking coffee from his favorite thermos with all the lights off, except maybe the stove light. He'd stare into the dark like you were just now. He'd say that he kept it dark so the light wouldn't wake me, but I think he just liked the calm of it."

"I like the calm of it, too."

"I figured as much."

"Do I look like him now?" I asked. I gazed into the

back yard, trying to imagine him doing the same. I held my cup and pretended it was coffee.

"More and more." She became very still and silent, not scratching my head or anything. Maybe she was holding her breath. Then she took my hand and rested it in hers. "I always thought you took after me and your sister, and I think that's still true. But now that you're getting older, I see him in the things that you do. The way you talk with your hands. Your feistiness. Lord, your father could be feisty sometimes. Never mean, though. He was never a mean man. Reminded me of your grandfather that way—he got hot, then he cooled right back down again. Everybody gets hot now and then, but it's the cooling off that matters."

I took a sip of water and laid my head back on her shoulder.

"Are you gonna marry Lou?" I asked.

She drew a sharp breath, and I thought maybe it was a laugh.

"It's not like that with us," she said. She was now talking in the faintest of whispers. My ears were still ringing from Lou's safe-cracking debacle and it was hard to make out what she was saying. "Besides, I know how you kids feel about him. Heck, sometimes I don't like him much either."

"Then why don't you kick him out?"

I regretted saying it. Mama shifted in her seat and she was no longer holding my hand, not scratching my head or anything. She'd stiffened up and let the blanket fall from her shoulders so we weren't in the same cocoon anymore.

"Well, sometimes a mom just needs help running things."

"I can help. Maisy and I can do anything."

"Sure. Anything but pay the bills."

I felt my body getting tense, too. If I could help pay the bills, I would do it in a heartbeat. I always pictured Maisy and I working down at the Boardwalk some day, waving to each other from our little steel boxes as we made the rides go around. We'd bring home our checks and Mama would be so proud. Between the three of us, we could make enough. There would always be paychecks floating through. We'd have to take turns going to the bank to deposit them all.

"I'm sorry, baby," she said. "I shouldn't have said that. School is your job. Just do well in school is all I ask." Her voice sounded monotone, as if she'd become distracted by another thought. She hugged me to her shoulder and her skin felt clammy. Whatever had shifted inside of her didn't seem to be going away.

There was a sound in the hall and another silhouette appeared. This one was large and round and brought with it the same kind of energy that Mama was suddenly giving off. This time, it wasn't much of a mystery. Lou watched us in the dark—and I could sense the look he was giving us without actually seeing it.

"What the hell's goin' on?" he said. There was a paranoid quality to his voice—he knew we'd been talking about him. "I thought somebody was breakin' in."

"Nobody's breaking in," said Mama. "Ben was getting a glass of water."

"A glass of what?"

"Water," I said. "The wet stuff that comes out of the sink."

The last part slipped from my lips before I had a chance to stop it. Maybe I was mad at myself for ruining a special moment with Mama, maybe I was just plain mad. Lou came closer, set his palms flat on the table. He was mostly naked, save for the tighty-whities that were partially hidden by the drape of his belly. He looked like an ogre from some low-budget fantasy flick. I could even hear his ogrish breath whistling in his nose.

"You sass-talkin' me again?" he hissed.

"I'll handle it," said Mama.

"You better. He's gonna think he can talk to everyone that way. Then he'll find out real quick what sass will get you."

"Go back to bed, Lou," said Mama. "I'll be right behind you."

"I told you he's got a mouth," said Lou. "I was just tellin' you."

"I'll talk to him."

He gave a hard stare with his hands splayed at his sides like he wanted to do something awful with them. I sipped my water and stared back, neither of us really able to see each other's eyes in the dark, just staring where the eyes should be. He cracked a bone in his neck with a quick tilt of the head, then he turned and stomped down the hall.

"You shouldn't mouth off to Lou," said Mama.

"He's got a worse mouth than anyone."

She placed her fingertips to her hairline and sat that way for a moment. I knew I'd made things worse for her somehow.

"Just do it for me, Benny. Do it because I asked you."

She rose and took my cup, poured out what was left in the sink. Then she took the afghan blanket and settled it over the couch so the stain wouldn't show.

"Well?" she said, standing with her arms crossed.

"Okay," I said.

"Okay, what?"

"I won't mouth off."

She cupped the back of my neck, guiding me out of the chair.

"Come on, tough guy," she whispered. "Try to get another hour of sleep before sunrise. It'll do you some good."

I followed her down the hall and watched her slip into the bedroom where Lou was waiting. He grumbled at her from behind the door and she whispered back, but I couldn't make out what they were saying. Something about me, no doubt.

I went to my room, where I could hear Maisy lightly snoring, her small form not even visible under the mound of blankets. What Mama told me didn't ring true. I couldn't see how sleeping could do me any good at all. Sleep wouldn't make Lou go away, wouldn't undo all the damage he'd done to our little family.

I planned on staring at the ceiling until everyone woke up and went about their business as I'd always done. But sleep found me unexpectedly, and I dreamed I was wandering through the redwoods with the fog so thick I could barely see from tree to tree. I stood with my fingertips touching the rough dry bark and tried to reach out to the next tree, one after the other in a gauzy maze. The last form I reached wasn't a tree at all, but a young woman holding a cat. I knew it was Jessie Barton, but I couldn't see her face well enough to tell if it was bloody or just like it was on the flyer. She held the cat out to me and I took it. I felt it purring in my arms, felt the warmth against my body, the whiskers brushing my face.

"What's his name?" I asked.

"His name is Ben," said Jessie, but with Mama's voice. "That's my name."

"I know," she said. "I named him after you."

10

IN THE LAST WEEK OF JULY, Maisy came to me in a panic. Mama was sleeping and couldn't be woken. She said she needed her to go to the store for something really important and if I could find Lou instead. I asked her what it was about but she wouldn't tell me. She nearly burst into tears before running into the bathroom and locking the door. I could hear her sobbing inside like something had gone really wrong. The way she looked at me with those big, scared eyes made me scared too. Mama and Lou were both a little messed up these days, but I could usually count on Maisy to stay cool.

I knocked on the bathroom door.

"You okay?" I asked. I knew she wasn't okay. She obviously needed help. But I didn't know what to say and Mama taught us to ask if someone was okay even when they seemed like they weren't.

"Just get Lou," she said.

"Why Lou?"

"Mama's got the flu doesn't she?"

I inched down the hallway a step or two and saw Mama curled under the window wearing nothing but a T-shirt and underwear, her body gently rocking with each breath. The wind rattled the blinds and a few strands of her blond hair wavered in the light. I called her name twice but she didn't respond.

"Yeah, she's got the flu all right."

"Then get Lou. Hurry."

I ran to the kitchen, but didn't find him there so I stood at the sink and looked through the window into the backyard. The grass stirred and the redwoods rolled in the sky. I went out the back and up the side of the house, and when I turned the corner I ran square into Lou's V-necked beer belly. It startled him as much as me. His fists curled and he took a step back in a fighting stance.

"You can't just ambush a man like that, boy. You're lucky I wasn't packin' heat."

"Maisy needs you," I said. "She's inside. In the bathroom."

He looked surprised, like he'd been sucker-punched. Then he rolled his eyes and crossed his arms. "She flushed one of them things, didn't she? Clogged the toilet?"

I told him she needed something from the store and he sighed and rolled his eyes again, sort of staggered back with his hands rubbing the back of his greasy neck in exasperation. "I don't got time for none of that shit, boy. I'm a busy man these days."

"It's just that—"

"Just what, boy?"

"Just—"

"Say it. Come on, *pussy nuts.*"

"I don't know. She won't tell me."

Maybe I'd pressed my luck too far. His face boiled and his eyelids seized over those beady black pupils. The eyes of an animal. Eyes that looked set to grow

teeth of their own and commence growling and snap-
ping. Those hard and menacing blue eyes reminded
me of some poisonous thing you'd find in the woods.
Maybe the flower book would help with something like
that. He softened unexpectedly and turned to his truck
in the driveway. He pressed the ball of his thumb to the
hood and dragged a dark furrow in the dust, clear from
one headlight to the other. He went inside, and when he
came out a minute later he told me to get the hose and
soap bucket ready.

"When I get back, you and your sister are gonna clean
my truck so shiny I'll be able to see it from space," he
said. Then he gave me a good hot stare and peeled onto
the road in a rush of white-blue smoke and sped away.

He wasn't long at the store. By the time I checked on
Maisy and Mama, fixed the garden hose to the spigot in
the front of the house, and filled a bucket with water and
soap like he'd shown us, I could hear that diesel engine
screaming back up the mountain toward home. He skidded into the driveway and hobbled out of the cab with a
lit cigarette between his lips, a little pink package in one
hand and a six-pack of Old Milwaukee clawed in the
other. He saw me standing with the hose and gave me a
quick nod as if giving the signal to commence spraying
the truck, but then he sort of skidded on his heels and
squinted at the left front tire, cocking his head.

"I'll be goddamned," he said. He spit out the cigarette and crouched down to get a better look. After a
moment, he called me over. "You see what the fuck I'm
looking at, son?"

I looked. The tire sagged, bulging over the lip of the
rim at the bottom.

"Is it flat?" I asked.

"Damn right it's flat," he said. "Next question is: *you know how much these tires cost?* I'll give you a beer if you guess right."

I didn't want a beer, but I knew he'd badger me until I said something.

"A thousand dollars?"

A grin spread over his face like a slow-moving disease. "The whole set would cost a grand. Maybe eight hundred. Divide it up and you got yourself about two hundred apiece. That's with the lifetime balancing and cut to the government. You think your mama makes that much in tips every day?"

I threw my hands in the air.

"I don't know, Lou."

"*I don't know Lou*," he parroted my words in a squeaky voice. "I got news, pussy nuts. Your Mama don't make jack shit at the diner. I'm just about financing this entire operation. Now I got to be the errand boy, too? And I run over a damn screw to top it off. You and your scrawny-ass sister better hope the shop can patch it up or you won't like what comes next."

He stomped into the house and I could hear him banging on the bathroom door, shouting at Maisy. The door opened and shut. I stood with the hose in my hand, trying to look useful. I stirred the bucket with the hose, filled it a little more. Foam volcanoed over the rim of the bucket. Lou came out the front door with a beer in one hand and a fresh cigarette in the other. Maisy stood behind him, expressionless. Just those brown eyes clicking from me to the truck and back again.

"Put that away for now," said Lou, nodding to the soap bucket. "Since you got no daddy, I'm gonna teach you both somethin' you ought to know. Somethin' most people don't even know how to do anymore." He brought us to the side of the truck and unlatched a bag of tools from beneath the seat of the king cab and chucked them onto the driveway with a metallic clatter. He slid the zipper down the bag, a jumble of steel and aluminum tools inside. He lifted a tire iron from the bag and handed it to Maisy. "Go ahead, now," he said, raising a finger to the wheel. "Break those nuts loose."

She held the tire iron with both hands. It looked so big in her hands, like something not meant for a child to hold. Her wrists weren't much wider than the tire iron itself. She knelt before the wheel and fumbled the thing onto the lugs and stepped back. We looked at Lou. He poured another mouthful of beer down his throat and watched us, shaking his head.

"Go on," he said.

She pulled the iron but it wouldn't budge. Didn't even make a sound. She tried harder, groaning. With both hands on it, she slipped and split her knuckles on the pavement. She jumped up, eyes wide. She shook her fingers in the air and danced in a circle, blowing on her hand. I saw the raw skin darken with blood.

"Hell," said Lou, clearly amused. "Maybe it's too much for you after all." He opened the truck door and from beneath the seat he pulled an aluminum pipe and tapped it in his hand. "You better use this breaker bar." He slipped the pipe over the handle of the tire iron and gestured graciously, as if doing us a big favor.

It took us the better part of an hour, both of us taking turns on the breaker bar, to crack each nut. The blood made the bar slippery, and that led to more knuckle-busters. We pleaded for a break, but he wouldn't cut us any slack at all. Not even for a drink of water. Then came the jack, and more wrenching. By the time we'd wrestled the spare into place and torqued the lug nuts, it seemed that every knuckle bled and throbbed, every muscle ached.

This wasn't a homeschool lesson on automobile maintenance.

It was corporal punishment, plain and simple.

Maisy didn't speak another word all night. When Mama finally woke, she found us in our room, sitting around a bowl of ice water with our hands submerged.

"What are you up to, sweeties?" She said it with a saccharine tone like everything was right in the world. She knew better, and I could see it in her face that she knew better, too. "Why the bowl?"

"Lou made us change his tire," I said.

Mama glanced out the window where she could see the truck.

"You helped him change a tire?"

"Nuh-huh," I said. "He made us do it all." I held up my hands and showed her. Knuckles purple and raw. I took Maisy's hands out of the water and lifted them up for Mama to see. Hers looked even worse. We looked like prize fighters from some underground league.

Mama took our hands in her own and blinked her eyes.

She crouched beside us for what seemed like an eternity. Sometimes her lips moved, but no words came. Just the tacky sound of her lips parting. Like a quiet prayer. Then she turned and left the room, shutting the door behind her. Our bedroom door didn't sit flush in the jamb, so to close it all the way, you really had to be committed. When she finally pushed hard enough to get that latch to click, Maisy and I gave each other a grave look.

There was going to be a fight.

Mama must have been whispering at first, because we only heard Lou rambling defensively. He told her about having to go to the store, trying to blame it all on Mama and Maisy. He said awful things about all of us. Then he stomped around the house, both of them yelling, screaming. Something crashed in the kitchen and it sounded like the silverware drawer emptied over the linoleum. The fight went on for another thirty minutes or so, and it might have lasted all night if Cowboy hadn't shown up when he did. Things cooled down for a few minutes, but then Lou and Cowboy started in on each other. It was like some switch had flipped in the center of the Earth and the whole world wanted to fight. They went outside and swore and yelled, calling each other things that we'd never heard before. Real bad words. Somebody slammed into the side of the house and the walls shuddered. It happened two or three times. Then, more curses and oaths. We saw Cowboy scamper past the bedroom window with blood on his mouth. He stomped to his truck, fired up the engine, and launched out of the driveway.

The rest of the night passed quietly. Mama came back with grilled cheese sandwiches and juice boxes. She refilled our bowl with ice cubes. She told us that we weren't in trouble, but that she wanted us to go to bed early because she wanted the house quiet. We did what she said, but Maisy now had a look that I couldn't read—something spinning and twisting in her mind. She sometimes had this silent rage to her, as if behind those hot eyes she sharpened things for use in future battles. I tried to get her to talk, but she only shook her head and blinked at the ceiling.

Just after midnight, I found out what she'd been

planning. I'd fallen asleep quickly, worn out from wrestling with that big old mud tire and from soothing my aching knuckles. I woke to find Maisy crouching in the dark, unzipping her backpack. She sat on the edge of her bed with a flashlight and slipped out her fifth-grade binder, thumbed through the papers inside. I lay with my eyes half-open, breath constant, trying to look asleep. She found Jessie Barton's flyer and set it in her lap, touched the picture with a single fingertip. I thought maybe she was stroking the image of the cat that lay in Jessie's arms.

Then she took the flyer and left the room. I heard the hallway creak as she went quietly into the front room, then the slight rattle of the front door handle. I got out of bed and went to the window. The horns of a crescent moon had just cleared the treetops, and I could see her slinking across the front lawn toward the driveway. She looked like some fairy tale creature flitting around in the moonlight. Like Peter Pan's shadow or a will-o'-the-wisp. Then she did something I didn't expect. Something I didn't think either of us were capable of. *Something calculated.* She went to Lou's truck, put her foot on the front tire and climbed up to the windshield. She whipped her head around, giving the house a quick look. I ducked, hoping she wouldn't see me. I don't think she did.

I popped my head up in time to see Maisy lift Lou's wiper blade and clip Jessie Barton's missing person flyer to the windshield.

11

I DON'T KNOW WHAT MAISY INTENDED, or what she thought would happen when Lou found what she'd done. Maybe she wanted him to know that someone had figured him out, that he wouldn't get away with it. Maybe she thought he'd leave town.

But Lou didn't leave, and he didn't cool down.

I knew the exact moment he discovered the flyer. It came with a bomb-blast of cusswords and a rampage so loud and violent I thought he would be heard all the way down the mountain. We watched from the window as he punched the air, kicked the bushes. He looked like the target of an angry swarm of wasps. Then he'd stop, look over the paper front to back, and get right back to kicking and screaming.

I thought he'd kill us for sure.

"Why'd you do that, Maisy?" I said. "I've never seen him so mad."

She looked startled, like she couldn't decide whether to deny it.

"You saw?"

"I watched you last night from the window."

The front door slammed and Lou stomped into the

living room. He must have flipped over the coffee table again. Big explosive clatter.

"I couldn't let him get away with it," she said. "It was mean what he did to us."

"You hear him, Maze? I don't think he'll ever calm down."

I heard Mama's bedroom door open, footsteps creaking down the hall. She asked Lou what this was all about with a summoned bit of confidence. He broke something else, I couldn't tell what. But amid all the ranting, a word came up again and again that put us at ease.

Cowboy.

Cowboy.

Cowboy.

He thought Cowboy had done it.

A few minutes later, Mama came into the room and told us to get dressed.

"You're coming to work with me," she said. "You can eat breakfast at the diner and hang out at the laundromat if you get bored."

We got dressed in a hurry. We didn't mind at all. Home was the last place we wanted to be, and we could smell the French toast already. Maisy grabbed her harmonica and I brought my sketchbook and pencils and we climbed into Mama's little Honda long before she came out with her work blouse and tennis shoes. We drove in silence down the mountain and into town. When we reached the Oak Street Diner, Mama fixed her makeup in the rearview and we followed her through the back door where the kitchen buzzed with the sounds of chopping knives, the whirl of industrial blenders. Campesino music blared from some hidden portable radio, and the smell of pie and bacon hung heavy in the air.

We sat in a corner booth and waited for Mama to clock in, deliberating over the menu even though we knew what we both wanted. I got the same breakfast every time: a stack of banana pancakes and hot chocolate. Maisy got French toast with whipped cream and a glass of milk. Mama didn't bring the food out for a long time. We heard her arguing in the kitchen with someone but we couldn't see who. After a while, she came out with our orders. Her eyes looked hard and a scowl clawed at her eyebrows. She couldn't even fake a smile. When she left again, I waited until she was out of earshot and I asked Maisy what she thought Lou would do to Cowboy.

"I don't care," said Maisy, with a mouthful of French toast.

"What if he beats him up again like last night?"

"So he beats him up."

"Looked like he got him good already."

She took a big sip from her cold glass of milk.

"Way I see it, the more time he spends beating up Cowboy, the more he'll leave us alone."

I rubbed my blood-crusted knuckles and nodded. I couldn't disagree with her about that. Maybe the trick was to keep him mad at Cowboy forever and we could just get on with our lives in peace. I poured a fountain of syrup over my banana pancakes and took a big bite, looking out the window as I chewed. The sun had cleared the tops of the redwoods and the light filtered through the glass, making little colored beams in the lacquer of the tabletop.

"You remember last time we were here?" I said.

It took her a moment to register what I said, but she

stopped chewing and gave me a long smile. "How could I forget about you and Miss California?"

"Stop it." I blushed. Miss California had stopped in as part of some press junket with the local school district and came to our table, tiara and sash worn just so. She looked like she'd stepped right off the stage of some prime-time beauty pageant. Like the whole world had been made just for her.

"She told you to look her up in Sacramento."

"I said stop it. She meant both of us."

"But she looked at you when she said it."

"Well," I couldn't hide it anymore. "She was pretty, wasn't she?"

"I guess," said Maisy. "If you like blue-eyed blondes with lots of makeup. Mama's prettier if you ask me."

I searched the room to make sure she wasn't listening. "Mama *was* prettier. Before Lou showed up."

"She's still pretty. Even with Lou around."

"But not like Miss California. Not anymore."

"How dare you. Take it back." She loaded a spoonful of whipped cream and catapulted it across the table, hit me square between the eyes. I scrubbed my face with a paper napkin and scooped what little whipped cream remained on my plate and returned a volley. I missed, the white spatter sinking down the wall behind her. It would have escalated to a full-blown food fight if Mama hadn't rushed over with her eyes wide and angry.

"You little monsters better cut it out," she said. "I'm this close to losing my job as it is." She toweled the whipped cream off the wall and gathered our plates, even though we weren't quite done. Maisy and I apologized at the same time, but she wasn't having it. "Go wash up in the bathroom and wait for me outside."

We did what she said, and when she came out again she looked even more flustered—on the verge of tears. She pulled her hair back tight, gave us a handful of quarters and told us to wait at the laundromat at the other end of the parking lot. It was an old building with a rusted metal sign that read EASY LOAD and catered mostly to folks who lived in the trailer park behind the shopping center. They had a few old arcade games and a TV that hung from the ceiling playing nothing but headline news.

It didn't take long to burn through the quarters. We sat on metal stools and watched news coverage of the presidential election, feet tapping the linoleum in a fit of boredom and whipped cream highs. It was Sunday morning, and the place bustled with townies. Maisy took out her blues harp and played a long riff up and down the comb. An old man with a wool hat stopped folding his laundry and turned to us.

"That sounded pretty good, kid." His whole face smiled. Big gray eyebrows angled up his forehead like he'd brushed them that way. "Let's hear another one."

She looked at me, blushing. I nodded and she put the blues harp to her lips and played again.

"She's good, isn't she?" I said.

The old man quickly agreed.

"She's not bad at all. I used to play a little myself, you know. Mostly down at the metro, sometimes in a band." He gave me a strange look as if trying to figure me out. "And what do you play, son?"

"Nothing. I'm her manager."

"Her manager?"

"That's right. I'm the one that booked this show."

The old man looked as though he were suddenly lost, eyes searching all around the place.

"Something's missing, kid."

"What?"

"You're the manager, you tell me."

Maisy grinned at this strange and befuddled man before us.

"Tell us," she said.

The man narrowed his eyes and unhatted my ball cap, looked it over as if he'd been searching for it all day.

"This is it. This is what's missing." He dropped it on the floor upside down and sorted a dollar from his bill-fold, creased it twice, and let it drop into the hat. "Keep playing, kid. Maybe someday you'll afford a fancier trailer than me." He went back to his laundry and tucked everything into his basket and shuffled out the door.

I picked up the dollar and unfolded it, straightened it against my leg.

"You thinking what I'm thinking?" I said.

She took the bill and turned it over.

"The Boardwalk?"

"We could go by ourselves. Catch the bus straight down the mountain."

Her eyes lit up.

"You think Mama would let us?"

"Maybe she would. Maybe we'd go when she's sleeping."

"If we got caught—"

"What would happen? These days, we could burn the house down and nobody would notice. They'd wake up, brush off the soot and pour themselves a cup of coffee."

"We never got to ride the Giant Dipper."

"Aren't you too small for that ride?"

"Not if I stand on my tiptoes."

She kept playing. She played every song she knew, and when she ran out of songs, she made up new ones. At times, a small crowd stood and listened, but mostly people came and went, tossing loose change and dollar bills into the hat as they passed. When the hat overflowed, I'd stuff what I could in my pockets and we'd start over. I couldn't believe how much money she was making. By the time Mama finished her shift, we had over thirty dollars in our pockets. We counted out every dollar and coin in the backseat of the Honda while Mama watched us in a sort of stunned amazement.

"I've had shifts where I made less than that," she said.

"Can we come back again tomorrow, Mama?" asked Maisy.

"We may have to." A dark line appeared between her eyes and she stared into her open hands for a moment. "You make more money than me now."

"What does that mean?" But I knew. Her eyes said it all.

"Don't be sad, little monsters. I saw it coming. The manager wanted me gone for a while now. I wasn't going to tell you right away, but we need groceries." She flicked her eyes at the busking cash that sat between us. We looked at the money and when we looked up again, a tear had cut a path down her cheek. "I know what you both think of me. I'm a terrible mother."

Maisy picked up the money and set it on the center console.

"It's our money," she said with a shrug. "For all of us. I can make more."

I had a couple dollar bills hidden away that suddenly

felt ice-cold against my thigh. I slipped out the money and laid it atop the stack.

"For all of us," I said.

Maisy flicked me on the shoulder.

"Thief."

"The manager gets a cut," I said. "Don't I?"

"Not anymore." She flicked me again, harder this time. "You're fired."

12

WE TALKED MAMA INTO BUYING cake mix and extra frosting at the grocery store. Under the circumstances, she wouldn't say no and we all knew it. Cake may have been the least we could get away with, but we were trying to be good sports about everything. It was Maisy's money, after all. We were debating whether to eat the cake for dinner or eat it for dessert when we pulled into the driveway and saw Cowboy's Ford Ranger parked in the garage. Mama cut the engine, hands on the steering wheel. Still as a stone. We watched the house in silence as if counting down to some imminent explosion, some destruct sequence that ticked in our bones.

"I don't hear any fighting," said Maisy.

Mama scratched the back of her neck, thinking.

"Maybe they already worked it out," she said. I pulled the door handle and got out, but Mama told me to hold on. "Let me go first," she said. She got out and glanced around the front yard as if expecting to find something there. "I'll meet you around back at the Grandfather tree."

"Yell if you need us," I said.

"No, you both listen to me," Mama said, her eyes flinty. "If you hear me yelling, I want you both to run into the woods and don't come out. I don't care how loud I scream and cry. Just run—both of you. *Understand?*"

We nodded, but Mama made us say it out loud.

We did.

She took an armful of groceries and went down the driveway while we tiptoed along the side of the house. The temperature flirted with triple digits, maybe the hottest day of the year. I could feel the heat rising up out of the dead grass. Beetles hummed through the air and a raven prattled nearby.

"You smell that?" Maisy said.

I lifted my nose in the air.

"Smells like a campfire."

"Yeah, but different."

When we turned the corner of the house, Maisy grabbed my shoulders and pulled me back. Down at the lower end of the property, Lou stood beside a raging burn barrel. Cowboy lay at his feet, face down in the grass and naked as a baby. A bloom of tangled hair rose from the back of his head like it had been styled that way. Blood caked his naked back and shoulders, a bloody shirt wadded beside him. Lou waved his hands as if to ward off smoke or flies. Maybe both. He dropped a pair of light blue Wrangler jeans into the fire.

We hurried back down the side of the house.

"Did he see us?" I asked.

"I don't think so."

"Was Cowboy—?"

She put her hands atop my shoulders and nodded, eyes wide.

"We have to tell Mama," I said.

"She told us not to go inside."

"She thought Lou was inside. Obviously he's not."

77

I didn't know what to do. I wanted Maisy to tell me. I wanted her to be the big sister. She looked to the backyard and she looked to the front, then she grabbed my hand and pulled me around to the front door. We found Mama in the front room with a soap bucket and an armful of cleaning rags. A mural of blood and stray hair soiled the wall above the woodstove, some of it dotting the ceiling like a starry constellation. The wind followed us through the door and it fluttered the hair caked on the walls.

Mama looked angry at first, but it quickly turned to fear—and some other look of shock or maybe panic.

"I told you to wait outside," she said. When she said it, I knew that panic was the correct emotion at work here.

"He's outside, Mama," I said. Now I sounded panicked too. I glanced at the dining table and saw a silver revolver with a white grip like you'd see in a Western movie. "We came back because, well." I almost couldn't say it. "Because Lou's in the backyard."

Her attention turned to the window and lingered there.

"Just wait in your room. I'll come get you when it's safe."

Maisy didn't like the idea.

"Why can't we just leave?" she said.

"Because it's our house," said Mama.

"But why can't we leave anyway?"

"Because we don't have anywhere to fucking go!" she screamed. Then, with her arm folded over her face so we couldn't see her eyes, voice breaking: "Just go."

We waited in our room for hours, just lying on our beds and listening to the sound of Mama scrubbing the walls. She'd stop every thirty minutes or so and smoke cigarettes in the front yard and we'd see the little gray puffs churn past the window. It gave me something to look at. Whenever I closed my eyes, I saw Cowboy face-down and bloody in the grass. I saw Lou throwing his clothes into the burn barrel. I couldn't stop thinking about it.

"Do you think he's going to burn Cowboy in that barrel?" I asked Maisy. It was the first thing we said to each other in an hour, and it took her a moment to answer.

"I don't know, Ben. I don't want to think about it."

"I don't either."

"Then stop."

"I can't. Why don't we just run away?"

"You heard Mama. We don't have anywhere to go."

"Maybe we do."

"Where?"

"Sacramento."

She swung her legs over the side of the bed and folded her arms, studying me carefully.

"You're talking about Miss California, aren't you?" She said it dismissively, like it was a stupid idea.

"She told us to look her up," I said.

"She didn't mean it."

"She hugged me and told me. She meant it."

"Okay. What's her name?"

"Her name?"

"We're just going to hitchhike to Sacramento and ask around for *Miss California?*"

"No. We're going to take the bus."

"I'm not taking a bus to Sacramento."

"Lou's going to kill us, Maze. He killed that Jessie lady and now he's killed Cowboy. Almost blew me up with dynamite a couple weeks back. He'll kill Mama and

79

then us. We've gotta get out of here. You even said so yourself."

"Keep your voice down."

"See. You're scared."

Maisy rubbed her face with her hands.

"I'll come with you, Ben," she whispered. "But not now. Not Sacramento."

"Then where? When?"

"I don't know. What about Mama? We can't leave her."

"If we leave, she'll come looking for us. It'll change things."

The floor creaked. Someone was coming down the hall. Mama opened the bedroom door and in her hands was the box cake, half-frosted with chocolate and the other half vanilla.

"I told you everything would be okay," she said. Her voice sounded dreamy and her eyes moved slowly. It looked like the Lou flu was coming on again. "Everything's okay when you have cake. Don't you think so?"

"Should we save a slice for Cowboy?" I said.

Maisy shot me an ice-cold stare.

"I don't know what you think you saw," said Mama. "Eat, now."

I felt my temper rising, blood pounding in my ears.

"Cowboy's not dead?"

"No, silly. Cowboy's not dead."

"Whose brains were you cleaning off the wall?"

"Stop it, Ben," Maisy hissed.

Mama set the cake on the desk and laid out a pair of forks and napkins.

"Eat," she said, crying now. "Just eat."

When she left, Maisy came up and slapped me.

"What was that for?"

"You know what. This is Lou's fault, not Mama's."

"She can kick him out anytime, can't she? But she doesn't."

"She's just scared like us. She's on our side."

"She doesn't kick him out and she doesn't leave. Is she really on our side?"

"Of course she is. Lou made her sick. We just have to help her."

It felt like we were going in circles.

"Help her how?"

"I don't know." She sat with her head in her hands.

"Either we run away, or we stay and kill Lou before he kills us all."

"Don't say that. And lower your voice. What if we call the police?"

"Won't they arrest Mama, too? It's her house, *her backyard.*"

"I don't know. Maybe."

"And they'd take us away, too. We'd be orphans."

"You're probably right."

"How much money do you have, Maze?"

She fished in her pocket and counted. "Fourteen dollars."

"Can I borrow it?"

"It won't get you far."

"I've got twenty of my own. I'll figure it out."

I cut us both a slice of cake with the butter knife Mama had left and slid them onto paper napkins. I poked my slice with the tip of my finger.

Raw in the center.

13

THE SHOVELING STOPPED around midnight. I lay all night wondering if he'd burned Cowboy's body and dug a hole for the ashes, or if the hole went deep enough for an entire unburned man. By the sound of it, he'd dug a very deep hole. I wondered how many graves the backyard could hold and what he'd do when he ran out of room. Where would he bury Maisy and me? Mama?

I heard Lou come in through the backdoor. The hallway creaked in that same noisy spot by the wall heater. Did he stop outside our bedroom? I imagined him with his ear pressed to the door, listening for movement. *Looking for witnesses.* Footsteps again. The sound of the shower handles chirping. Water flowing. I'd already stuffed my school backpack with a change of clothes, a blanket, and an empty canteen. I kept a flashlight under the bed and I packed that too.

Shoes.

Beanie.

Jacket.

Go.

"No. Don't go," Maisy's silhouette whispered.

I paused at the door.

"I already made up my mind."

"The road's not safe at night. You'll get hit by a truck, just like Jessie."

"I'm not taking the road. I'm gonna follow the creek all the way into town."

She didn't respond, just a thin and silent form stamped against the moonlit window.

"I've got to get out of this place, Maze," I said. "Come with me. Please."

Still nothing.

I heard her settle back into the bed and I turned to leave.

The knob turned quietly enough, but the door groaned when I pulled it. I waited, listening. The shower ran. Lou took long showers. Maybe it took longer for bad people to get clean. Maybe it was harder to get gravedirt out of your fingernails than the regular kind of dirt. I went down the hall, careful of the noisy spot in the carpet. The dining room smelled like every kind of household cleaner at the same time. I glanced where the blood stain had been. It appeared when I blinked my eyes, like the stain had become haunted.

At least we'd have plenty of ghost stories to tell.

Lou had forgotten to close the sliding door and I slid the screen and stepped into the moonlight. The crescent moon hung low and bright in the trees. I could see all the way across the backyard to the woods. The air smelled of pine needles and cold grass. I cinched the straps of my backpack and trudged down the sloped yard, over the squirrel holes and patches of dry weeds. Over the dynamite scar. I crossed the bald spots in the earth where Lou's old bumper lay buried in pieces with Jessie's hacksawed bicycle. I gave the burn barrel a kick and two lazy sparks coiled up into the night and winked out. I went past the fresh plot of gravedirt where Cowboy's ashes or some other remnant of him lay. At the treeline, I heard the burble of the creek. A sound like tiny crystals. Here, forget-me-nots blued over a patch of disturbed soil. I clicked my flashlight and swept the ground.

Another grave plot.

I'd found Jessie Barton.

Little blue flowers catching the starlight.

Little blue flowers whispering secrets of the dead.

I went through a bramble of wax myrtles and came out onto the gritty creekbed. Not much water at all. I clung to the banks and stepped slowly downstream, slipping on the stones but never falling. The wind had picked up and it blew down the mountain, a stench of minerals and moldering things. It bothered the bay laurels, branches hissing and grinding, dead summer leaves tumbling all around me. After a while I came upon an abandoned footbridge and I climbed atop to see how far I'd come, but I only saw the night sitting atop the creek-stones, the moon's warped reflection in the tiny stream. It could have been a mile or just a few hundred yards. It was just so hard to tell. The water clinked and whorled under the footbridge, winding toward town and onward to the sea. For the first time I realized that some things only flowed one direction and never looped around again. You move ahead and the weight of the universe rolls with you. It swallows up the past. If I turned back, it wouldn't be the same house and I wouldn't be the same kid. I could almost feel it change. Some fork had split and I now walked through an entirely different world.

I unzipped my backpack and draped the blanket over my shoulders. The creek grew wider. Fallen redwoods angled over the water. At some points, the bank tightened and it took time to hop from stone to stone, clambering over logs, zig-zagging the creek. After another hour, my legs grew tired. I came out along a sandbar and crouched by the water, shined the flashlight up and down the stream.

Something shined back.

A pair of eyes.

I stepped away from the water with my back pressed to the trunk of a large bay laurel. A form slipped into the trees and disappeared, and another appeared at the far end of the bank. Dark and quiet, eyes yellow in the beam of light. Another appeared. I knew what they were even before the first excited yip. We'd seen coyotes along the creek before, but at a distance. In the daytime they skittered along the creekbed, nervous and fearful. But this was their time to be bold. Their time to drag dead fawns from midnight backyards. *To hunt and devour.* I didn't know whether to run, hide, or fight them. I circled the tree trunk. Another yip. Scampering in all directions. Maybe they'd be afraid of a grown man, but they'd clearly sized me up and decided it was worth the effort. I stuffed the flashlight in my jacket pocket and straddled the bay laurel. The trunk arced over the creek like the long neck of a dinosaur, the angle just shallow enough to inch along with everything I had. I wasn't getting very far and every joint in my body felt electrified with panic.

I screamed for help, screamed so loud my voice cracked.

I climbed another inch. My foot slipped and dangled off the tree and I felt the night dogs tug back, whining and panting. My shoe peeled off and landed in the creekstones and I quickly returned my foot to the trunk. The animals scurried in a frenzy. I reached a small shoot and grabbed hold and pulled myself higher, then used it to push off with my feet when I passed it. I looked down. I perched six feet off the ground now, maybe more. I screamed again, screamed with the same intensity as the day at MacLeod's chop shop. I growled and spat. Something about my voice scared me. Like the forest knew my screams and listened back ghoulishly. The sounds of prey, of death—the bleat of a gutted fawn. The forest knew my role. Somewhere other creatures listened too. Watchful and curious. Waiting their turn at the kill. Such was the business of predators and scavengers.

But sometimes the prey escapes.

The tree branched off and I slipped my hand into the split and pulled. The blanket had fallen from my shoulders and I now felt the cold air on my sweat-damp neck. I zipped the jacket tight and pulled my beanie low, curling into the fork of the branch with my chin tucked. I waited. After a long while, their little forms scampered into the brush. Every now and then a gust would blow down the ravine and the branch buoyed up and down, bay leaves rattling, their smell vaguely medicinal.

Sometimes I'd fall asleep and wake up shivering. I listened to the forest sounds and I thought of Maisy's story about the mud children crying in the dark, eyes spilling with mud and blood. Was the moon full? No, not quite. But tonight, the mud witch wouldn't need to stalk the streets looking for children to flay. Tonight, I'd come to her.

When the shivering stopped, I slept again. I didn't dream of witches or mud children or coyotes. I dreamed of Miss California. I dreamed that I'd found her and she took me in and made me hot chocolate. Big pretty smile like she'd been waiting all that time. She lived in a house full of flowers and windows. She made an extra mug of chocolate for Maisy, and I placed it on the windowsill so that she could follow the smell and find us all the way from that nightmare house in the mountains.

14

I WOKE TO A CHANGING SKY. A cold gray light in the tree-tops. Crows soared by the hundreds from their night roosts. Sometime during the night, I'd buried myself in the spare clothes from the backpack. I wore socks on my hands like a poor man's mittens. I could see where the blanket fell onto the bank of the creek and I slowly scooted down the sloped trunk after it. My shoe lay half in the water, shoelaces frayed and tongue akimbo. Little dimples in the leather where the coyotes had laid their jaws.

Were they still watching? Or were they now timid in the daylight?

I wrapped the blanket tightly around my shoulders but I still couldn't get warm. A dead maple lay crooked over the creekbed and I gathered dry branchlets from its crown and piled them onto a sandbar. I dug a shallow pit and crisscrossed the kindling and lit it with Lou's tattered gas station lighter. The fire crackled and sputtered. I found more dead wood to add. I planted sticks in the sand beside the fire and piked my shoes over the tips and I ate a granola bar I had stashed away in my coat pocket. My face and hands warmed quickly. Maisy would be so proud. The coyotes, the night in the tree. The blazing campfire. Next time, I'd tell her a better story, and this time it would all be real.

The fire grew.

I circled it, dodging the flames. Twisting and dancing.

If they could only see me.

With the sun yet to clear the treetops, I toed into my warm shoes and continued down the creek in the direction of town. I made much better progress in the daylight, leaping from one bank to the other, hopping along the granite stones. At one point, the creek swelled to a large pool, too deep to cross. I had to climb up the embankment and follow a deer trail into the waist-high rattlesnake grass. The path widened and connected to a well-worn footpath that wound through giant redwood trees and swathes of green sorrel. Trillium glowed in the tree shadows, gold stamens and phantom white pedals. Salmon-colored fungus scalloped on the redwood bark like elven footholds. For a moment I wished I'd brought my wildflower guide, but I knew carrying it would have been a hassle, although one good toss at a coyote snout would probably send it scampering with its tail tucked.

I passed through an overgrown backyard. A wilt-ed-looking house with dead windows and an old dog tied to a tree, belly pressed to the dirt. The dog saw me and barked but didn't get to its feet. I woofed back. Maybe it knew how I'd fought off its wilder cousins. I straddled a crooked fence and entered another yard, then another. The houses grew taller and more expen-sive. So did the fences, now unscalable. In the yard of a two-story stucco house, I spotted an open gate, a road just beyond. I crouched along the fence, past a garden shed and a row of compost bins. A few feet from the gate, a blond-haired boy poked his head over the back porch.

"Who are you?" said the boy.

I stopped, thumbs in my shoulder straps.

"I'm just cutting through," I said.

"Through from where?" He looked at me like I'd leapt from the pages of some book of fairy tales. "From the forest?"

"That's right," I said. "I came down the creek from the mountain."

He blinked into the distance, trying to picture it.

"Are you running away?"

I hesitated.

"Yes."

"Where to?"

"Someplace far away."

Something crashed inside the house and a man's voice roared. Another child screamed. More clattering, then more screaming.

"I want to come with you," said the boy in a half-whisper.

I looked through the open gate. A blue car passed on the street beyond.

"You can't. I'm going a long way." I took a step.

"Wait."

I waited.

"How do you run away?" he asked. "Tell me how."

Tears clung to his lashes. He looked frightened.

"Do you have a backpack?" I said.

He nodded quickly. "Every kid has a backpack."

"Just fill it with clothes and food. And bring a canteen of water."

"That's all?"

"Well, you'll need money for the bus, too. But once you've taken it as far as you can, you'll be in another city. That's basically it."

"I'll go to Hollywood," he said. "My mother's a movie star, you know. She's been in all the big action movies. Every single one. Once she sees how big I've grown, she'll know I can take care of myself and she'll let me live with her again. When I'm a little older, I'll come back for my brother, Johnny. We'll all be movie stars together."

The sliding door flew open. Heavy footsteps on the patio.

A deep, angry voice: "Who the hell are you talking to, Danny?"

Danny shrieked and spun on his heels.

I sprinted through the gate.

I ran past houses with green lawns and bicycles ditched on the driveways, past old ladies walking even older-looking dogs. Eyes followed me suspiciously at each turn in the road. I followed the street until it connected with a busier street and then I took that street to the center of town. Lumber trucks trundled through the intersections, spitting black exhaust. Smaller cars wound through the morning traffic. A little donut shop sat on the corner. The smell from the open door sweetened the air. My stomach ached with hunger, but I knew that every dollar I spent on food wouldn't get me quite as far away from home. I felt the wad of cash in the toe of my front pocket. Only thirty-four dollars. I glanced at the menu taped to the donut shop window and worried how little money thirty-four dollars amounted to.

I went another block until I found a bus stop with a green bench and route information mapped onto a sign. I sat, rolled my head side to side. One thing about sleeping in the crook of a tree branch is that it leaves your muscles feeling wooden too. In the small pocket of my backpack I found an apple I'd picked from one of the neighborhood trees and I took a bite. I hadn't yet studied the bus route, but I didn't want to yet. I was content to sit and watch traffic, eating my apple and waiting for that big blue bus to meander down the way.

After a few minutes, a little red Toyota convertible pulled up to the bench and the driver lowered his sunglasses.

"That you Ben?"

I sat up, studied the man.

It was Don Halbert, my school principal.

"Oh, hey Mr. Halbert," I said. As much as I didn't want anyone to find me, it was good to see a friendly face. He cut the engine and came around to the front of the car, sat on the hood.

"You just resting, or are you waiting for the bus?" He folded his arms over his belly and stood with his feet crossed as if he were posing for a photograph and trying to look cool.

"Well, I'm waiting for the bus, to be honest."

"All by yourself?"

"I'll be eleven soon if you didn't know."

"Heck, bud. I know you can handle a little bus ride by yourself, just that this one takes you all the way down the mountain to Santa Cruz. It doesn't even run till noon."

I folded my arms and crossed my feet like him.

"Yeah, I know," I said. "Just didn't want to miss it is all."

Halbert laughed.

"Oh, you won't. You got three hours to spare."

"Three hours?"

"That's right." He eyed my backpack and flashed a big friendly smile. "Everything okay, Ben?"

I didn't respond, just took another bite of my apple and chewed. The stoplight changed and a motorcycle gunned down the street. An old man on the corner covered his ears and watched it go by, mouthing a cuss word.

Halbert spun the car keys on his finger.

"Tell you what," he said. "I don't know about you, but I could eat a horse. I'm going to pull around back and get a bite at this donut shop. Feel like a donut and some chocolate milk? Looks like you have plenty of time to kill."

I had every intention of saying no. My head even started to shake side to side a little. But my stomach took the lead and decided a shrug was the best response. Truth is, I was ravenous. The apple tasted as sour as a lemon. But there was also a part of me that wanted to tell him about last night. About the coyotes and the bay laurel tree. How I'd started my own campfire. I figured of all the kids he'd known through the years, he'd surely never heard of something like that.

When I told him, he just nodded his head like he'd heard it all before.

I thought he didn't believe me, so I showed him the bite marks on my tennis shoes. How my clothes reeked of woodsmoke. He nodded and chewed, sipped his coffee. Just listening to me talk. I wondered if it was a tactic to get me to tell him everything I was hiding.

If so, it was working.

"All that's pretty brave of you," Halbert said. "But I'm worried about the next part of this adventure. You think coyotes are dangerous? Wait till you see downtown Santa Cruz. We're in the middle of a drug epidemic if you hadn't heard about it. Tons of meth and heroin on the streets right now. A kid like you, even a tough kid like you, is likely to disappear in all that madness. Men are the worst animals of them all."

"I'm not staying downtown," I said, chewing.

"Then where are you headed?"

I needed a sip of chocolate milk to swallow the wad of maple donut at the back of my throat.

"You remember last year when Miss California came to town?" I said.

Halbert nodded.

"I remember. She visited the school to talk about some science scholarships for the girls."

"I saw her at Mama's diner, too. My Mama works at— *used to work at*—the Oak Street Diner. Miss California came in for breakfast and that's when she told me to look her up next time I visited Sacramento."

"So you're headed to Sacramento?"

"That's right."

"To see Miss California?"

"Yes sir."

"Does she know you're coming?"

"Nope."

He looked very perplexed with his eyebrows crooked and lips rolled to one side of his mouth. "Tell me, son. What do you think will happen when you knock on that door?"

"Well, I guess she'd answer and invite me in."

"Then what?"

"Then she'd offer me something to eat and we'd get to talking. Eventually, she'd set me up in one of her rooms and let me stay with her for a while. Maybe forever. Someday I'd marry her and make her *Mrs. California.*"

Halbert laughed at this.

"You're very young to be thinking about marriage," he said.

"She's pretty though, isn't she?"

"Hell, son. You don't win beauty contests if you're ugly."

I stuffed the last bite of maple donut into the pocket of my cheek.

"What time is it now?" I asked.

He looked at his watch, shook his wrist.

"We've been sitting here about twenty minutes is all. Could you eat another donut?"

"I could try," I said, and in a short minute I had before me the most glorious cinnamon twist I'd ever seen.

Halbert waited for me to take a bite and then he swished his coffee in his mug. He gave a sober expression.

"Now Ben, I got some news and I don't think you'll like it."

"What kind of news?"

"Well, it's about Miss California. Son, do you know what month it is?"

"July, isn't it?"

"That's right, July 25th. We're crowding August now. Do you know what happens in July?"

"Fireworks. The Fourth of July."

"Sure. But they also crown a new Miss California. Buddy, that woman you met isn't even Miss California anymore. By now she's just some Stanford or Berkeley grad student gearing up for fall semester. Dollars to donuts, she's dating some junior partner at a Silicon Valley tech firm with a cocaine problem and a malignant ego. Maybe he doesn't even like her very much, but dating last year's Miss California is boosting his reputation within his dating pool. Six months from now, she'll cheat on him with her Latin American Literature professor, and he'll cheat on her with anything that moves." He leaned forward and tousled my hair. "I know we're talking like adults here. Point is, Ben, we're all just regular people. When she won that competition, she got to be a beauty queen for a while. But now she's just little Sally Hicks from Bakersfield or wherever. Nobody will even recognize her. I know that bursts your bubble but just imagine how she must feel right now. She got to borrow fame for a bit and then she had to give it up."

I felt sick. Maybe it was the second donut.

"Is her name really Sally Hicks?" I asked.

"No, son. I just made that up. I was making a point."

"Who won, then?"

"You mean the pageant?"

"Yeah. Who's the new Miss California?"

"Some other blonde from San Diego, I think. Looks just like the last one."

"San Diego, huh?"

"Don't even think about it, Ben. Now this all leads me to the big question I need you to answer. I've been straight with you so far and I hope you appreciate it. It's time for you to be straight with me now. Can you do that?"

I didn't answer at first, just gazed out the window. A homeless man shuffled by, kicking a shopping cart full of junk along the sidewalk. Mottled, leathery skin. He cupped his hands to the glass and swept the room with haunted eyes as if looking into the past. Taped to the window was a flyer for Jessie Barton, this one with a different photo and a new reward amount of thirty thousand dollars. I stood up and pulled the flyer from the glass and sat back down, looking it over very intently.

"How do you go about claiming this reward?" I asked him.

Halbert gave a long sigh through his nose.

"Do you know what happened to that girl?"

"Maybe I do."

"Look, son. I asked you to be straight with me."

"Well." I spoke softly, looked around the donut shop to see who might be listening. "What if someone buried her in my backyard?"

Halbert sat back in his seat, folded his arms.

"Well, I guess you could claim the reward if you told the cops about it. You and your imaginary girlfriend could live off the money for a few months and then you'd have to find some other missing girl to cash in on." His words felt sharp, biting. Then he softened a little. "That was wrong of me, kid. I'm sorry. I just need you to be straight with me like I said. Tell me what you're really running from. That's all. That's what I need to hear."

"Lots of things, I guess." I felt defeated. I just told him the darkest secret I could imagine and he didn't even believe me. No wonder people stayed missing forever.

"Lots of things? Give me two things."

"Well, Mama's been sick."

"Sick how?"

"She just sleeps all the time. Ever since Lou came into the picture."

"Who's Lou? Her boyfriend?"

"I guess you could call him that. Lou would be the second thing."

"Does Lou hurt you?"

"Well, not in so many words."

"That's not an answer, Ben."

I didn't realize I was crying until the tear cooled my chin.

"Not directly."

"Still not an answer."

"He mostly hurts other people."

"Like your sister and mother?"

"No. Mostly people I don't know."

Halbert nodded calmly, patted me on the shoulder.

"Here's how this is going to go, son. And I'm sorry, but you only have two options here. Either we go to the police and you elaborate on exactly who Lou is hurting, or I take you home and try to work this out with your mother. But I'm not going to let you catch a bus out of town to Sacramento or anywhere else, understand?"

The tears flowed uncontrollably now, and the lady behind the counter looked me over with a sad expression of her own. She gave Halbert a nod and he nodded back. Part of me wanted to run through the door and keep running, but I didn't have a plan anymore. Nowhere to run. I didn't want to go to the police and I didn't want to go home. Yesterday I felt so driven, so certain. Now I felt like a helpless child again. I thought of Maisy, waking up all alone in that god awful place. I knew she worried about me, and I worried about her too.

Maybe I'd been wrong.

Sometimes you do move backwards.

"Take me home," I said. "Just don't expect Mama to come to the door."

15

WE WERE HALFWAY up the mountain when I asked Halbert to pull over.

He gave a quick nod and wheeled the Toyota onto a long dirt pull-out. We'd just passed Hopkins Gulch where the right lane had crumbled into the creek during the last winter storm. Halbert eyed me warily as if he expected me to jump out and make a run for the creek. He kept the car running.

"Do you have a piece of paper I could write on?" I asked.

"In the glovebox. Help yourself."

I found a pad of school stationary and a cheap fountain pen and I scribbled down an address on Keller Drive.

"There's a kid here that I want you to check on. I think maybe he's in trouble and I might have given him some bad advice."

Halbert repeated the address like he knew the place.

"Is that all?"

I set the pad in the glovebox and shut it.

"Well, that and I want you to remember what I said about that missing girl."

"That she's buried in your backyard."

"That's right, and she's not the only one. I want you to remember, in case, you know, anything happens to us."

Halbert had kept up the principal role since he'd found me at the bus stop. Friendly, calm. Somewhat stern. For the first time, his expression broke and he now had the look of an unsettled man. He didn't give a response, just stared up the mountain as if working the angles in his mind. He checked the mirrors and wheeled slowly onto the road.

He was starting to believe me.

When we reached the house, Halbert parked along the road. Lou's truck sat in the driveway next to the Honda. Someone had left the garage door open but I didn't see anyone about.

"You can go," I said. "You don't have to come in."

Halbert had already opened the car door.

"That wasn't the deal, bud." He stepped out and motioned for me to come along. He followed me across the lawn to the front door. With any luck, Mama would still be asleep and Maisy could help me get rid of him before Lou spotted us. I'd barely got the door open before Maisy rushed through and wrapped her arms around me. She didn't say anything at first, just hugged me tight and swayed back and forth.

"Hello Maisy," said Halbert. "Your mother home?"

She glanced over her shoulder into the dark of the house.

"Sorry, she's asleep."

Halbert glanced at his watch.

"It's noon. Your mother usually sleep this late?"

Maisy and I searched each other's faces for answers.

"I told you she was sick," I said.

"You said she got sick when this fellow arrived, Lou

was his name?" Halbert pressed into the doorway, glancing about the front room. I could swear that his eyes lingered over the faint stain on the wall. "Is Lou home?"

"Lou's working on something in the backyard and doesn't want to be bothered," said Maisy. She pulled me through the door and blocked Halbert with her slight body. "Thanks for bringing my brother back. I'll let Mama know you wanted to talk to her."

"Now hold on," said Halbert. He widened his stance and folded his arms, summoning his principal persona. "I found Ben here on a bus stop heading to Sacramento. I need to straighten this out with an adult. Doesn't that sound reasonable?" He took another step into the house, peering down the hallway.

Maisy held up her hands.

"Just leave your number. She'll call, I promise."

"You said Lou was in the backyard?" Halbert went to the kitchen and looked through the sliding door. "Can I go out this way?"

We took Halbert by the hand, pulling him toward the front door.

"You really don't want to bother him, Mr. Halbert," I said.

"Actually, I do want to bother him." He pulled his hands free and slid the glass door, stepped onto the dead grass. We followed close behind.

I spotted Lou backing out of the tool shed with a can of WD-40 and a dirty shop rag in his hands. A weedwacker lay on a ragged blue tarp, disassembled in a half dozen pieces. When he saw us, he froze. Shoulders back, mouth hung in a tight frown. He looked like a man about to throw a punch.

"Who the fuck is this guy?" said Lou.

Halbert had the determined look of authority about him. "I'm Don Halbert, the principal at the elementary school. I'm here about Ben." He offered his hand, but Lou didn't take it.

"Who let you into my house?"

Halbert didn't have an answer for this.

"I let him in," said Maisy. "He just wanted to talk to Mama."

"I don't give a good goddamn what he wants," said Lou. Then to Halbert: "I ain't this boy's daddy so I don't give a good goddamn about him either. Get lost."

"Now hold up, Lou." Halbert said. He had his fingers splayed, tapping the air as if it would somehow cool everything down. "There's a matter we have to discuss. See, as a school administrator, I'm a mandated reporter. Do you know what that means?"

Lou's face turned a blotchy red. He set the WD-40 on the workbench next to his glass pipe and tossed the rag over it. His jaw ratcheted back and forth as if he were chewing on something he couldn't break down. He pointed his finger to the road.

"Get the fuck off my property. I won't ask again."

"You better listen to him, Mr. Halbert," I said. Maisy pressed her shoulder into mine, held my hand tight. "Just do what he says. Please, Mr. Halbert."

Halbert took a step back.

"All right, fair enough. I'll go. But something's going on with these kids. They're scared. We have unfinished business here."

Lou stomped his foot and swiped a fist in the air.

"Like hell we do," he growled.

Halbert turned to leave, spinning his keys on his finger. He stopped before he turned the corner into the side yard and gave Lou a long, speculative look. Then he said something he shouldn't have. Something that set our entire world on fire.

"You ever heard of a woman named Jessie Barton?"

Lou looked like he'd been made a fool.

"Can't say I ever have."

"Went missing around here not too long ago," said Halbert. "It was all over the news."

Lou gave a quick shrug, jaw tightening.

Halbert offered a grim parting glance.

"Stay safe, kids. I'll check on you soon." He rounded the side of the house and disappeared down the side yard.

Lou went after him.

A coil of trimmer line from the weedwacker hung in his hands.

Maisy and I pleaded: *"No, Lou. Please, Lou! Don't do it."*

It happened quickly. Halbert was a half-foot taller, but Lou knew how to take down a taller man. He'd been doing it his whole life. They toppled against the side gate, grappling and punching. Halbert tried to reason with him but Lou wouldn't let up. He'd become an animal, growling and hissing. Just like the man I saw at the junkyard a few weeks back. I pictured him in a hundred different midnight truck stops, dragging a hundred different men to the asphalt, fighting until every last bit of rage emptied or got beaten out of him. Sometimes winning, sometimes losing, but always with that blind animal fury.

Halbert cried out. Lou hurt him bad somehow. He flipped Halbert onto his stomach and slipped the trimmer line around his throat. Fists balled, wrists crisscrossed and shaking. Every muscle knotted up.

"Go wake Mama," I said to Maisy. "Drag her out of bed if you have to."

"Okay, but don't do anything stupid, Ben."

"Just go."

She disappeared into the house, and I went to the blue tarp and scooped up the weedwacker, choked it up like a baseball bat. When I reached Lou, he had the trimmer line taut, sweating and grunting. Halbert convulsed beneath him, urine spreading in a pool over the paving stones.

I don't remember what I screamed at him. It must have been something wild, because for a moment Lou had a shocked look in his eye. *Fear-stricken.* I brought the weedwacker down across his back and he howled and cussed. He didn't let go of Halbert, though. I raised my arms for another blow, but he rocked forward and bicycle-kicked me in the gut. The kick sent me reeling against the side of the house and the weedwacker clattered to the ground. My breath caught in my chest. I heaved and choked, and by the time my breath returned, Lou started to get up again.

We locked eyes.

Trimmer line in his hands.

I scrambled to my feet and ran.

I found Maisy in Mama's room, trying to get her to wake. I closed the door and thumbed the lock, my breath fast and hard like I'd just run a dozen miles.

"Is she waking up?" I asked.

She didn't reply. She had Mama sitting forward on the bed, patting her cheeks. In the covers sat a hypodermic needle and a metal cap with a brown-looking cottonball inside. Mama groaned, eyelids barely parted. Hair matted to one side.

"We need to get out of here, Maze," I said. "He killed Mr. Halbert."

"He's dead?"

I nodded with eyes full of tears.

"Mama's really sick," she said. "We can't leave her like this."

"We'll get help."

"Which way do we run?"

"We can take the creek to town. I did it last night. Come on, Maze." I pulled her toward the door, but she froze. The doorknob jiggled, then rattled.

A loud crash.

The door burst open in a hail of pinewood splinters. Lou stood in the doorway, a shovel in each hand.

"You killed your own school principal, boy." He spat on the carpet and shook his head slowly. "*Heartless.* Then you tried to kill me, too."

"I didn't kill nobody, Lou." We backed deeper into the room until our backs pressed to the wall.

"You sure as shit did. The moment you told him about that Barton girl."

"I didn't tell him nothing."

"Don't lie to me, pussy nuts. Maybe it was you that put the flyer on my windshield after all. Did you get Cowboy killed, too?" He tapped my chin with the blade of the shovel.

Maisy batted it away.

"Don't touch him with that thing," she growled.

"Or what? You two don't have a friend between you in this lonely ol' world." He had both shovels pressed to our throats, now. "Once you help me clean up this damn mess, we'll talk about your punishment. One thing's for damn sure, it'll be about as bad as can be. Trust me on that. But first, I want you to dig a hole for your chubby ol' friend."

"Lou, what's all this?" Mama mumbled, coming to.

"Your boy made a mess, Carolyn."

"He killed Mr. Halbert, Mama," I cried. "The school principal."

Her head tilted, eyes squinting. Trying to make us out through the cobwebs. For a moment, her gaze seemed to sharpen and we locked eyes—but she softened again and went someplace else, someplace inward.

"You better help him clean up, Benny," she said.

"Mama, he's dead! Don't you hear me?"

She sank into the pillows, eyes fluttering. Asleep again. We yelled for her to wake up, but she only lay there, lightly moaning.

"Come on, kids. You heard your sweet mama." Lou stepped into the hallway and motioned with his chin. I never thought blue eyes could look so sharp and mean. "This grave ain't gonna dig itself."

16

LOU PLANTED HIMSELF IN A LAWN CHAIR with a trio of Coors tallboys, his faux ivory-handled cowboy gun laying on the ground at arm's reach. He drank and barked orders. It took us a few minutes to get Halbert onto the blue tarp, and once we did, we dragged him down to the trees where Lou wanted us to dig. He seemed to enjoy watching us struggle with Halbert's body. The first few shovel loads came up easily, but soon the ground became mostly clay and the work slowed down. Flies corkscrewed the air, drawn to the smell of the newly dead.

We found that if we stood with our backs to Lou, we could whisper undetected.

"We can run," I said. "He wouldn't catch up."

"He'll shoot us. He's watching too closely."

"If we use the shovels like shields, we could make it."

"That's way too risky. I've got a better idea." She dug another load and dumped it in the pile, whispered: "Isn't Mr. Halbert's car parked on the road?"

"Yeah, so?"

"If you were Lou, wouldn't you want to get rid of it before someone notices he's here? It might give us some time, even if he just moves it into the garage."

"He'll know we're up to something, won't he?"

"No, watch this." She turned to Lou and pointed at Halbert's corpse. "Do you want his car keys before we bury him?"

Lou straightened, rubbed at his neck. Wheels turning.

"Bring 'em here," he said. "And his wallet."

Maisy went through Halbert's urine-soaked pocket and produced a crowded ring of keys. Then she found his wallet and handed Lou both items, wiping her hands on her jeans. He went through the billfold and pulled out a handful of twenties, stuffed them in his back pocket. He'd already drunk all three tallboys, and when he stood, he took a moment to find his balance.

"Listen up, dipshits," he said, standing over us. He fished a cigarette from a battered hardpack in his front pocket and held it unlit at the corner of his lips, wedged the gun down the back of his pants. "We've got a new plan."

I stopped digging. Maisy and I exchanged glances.

"Skinny-legs stays and digs a proper hole. Boy, you come with me."

"Where are we going?" I asked.

"The next time you ask, it'll be your ass. Got it?"

"Yes sir."

"That's more like it. You stirred up some real shit here, boy." He lit his cigarette and blew the drag over Halbert's body. Then, to Maisy: "Don't you think of trying anything. If we come back and you're gone, you won't ever see your prissy little brother again. We clear on that? And if that hole's not deep enough, it'll be one of you that goes in it."

He motioned for me to follow him and we left Maisy standing over the hole. Lou paused at the Grandfather tree and took a long, grunting piss and went out through the side yard to the front of the house where he found Halbert's Toyota parked on the road. He popped the trunk and found nothing inside but a pile of gym clothes and an empty water bottle. He opened the passenger door and emptied the contents of the glovebox onto the seat. It hurt to see the note I'd written Halbert, the one with the boy's address.

Maybe the kid would make it to Hollywood.

Maybe he'd never make it to junior high.

Lou hit the ignition and put his foot into the pedal, racing the engine with the car in neutral. He shook his head like the sound insulted him somehow. The way he held the steering wheel, you'd think it was made of dog turds.

"Goddamn rice rockets," he said. "The kind of man who drives a car like this deserves a choke-out." Then he looked at me, said: "Now would be the time to buckle the fuck up."

I'd barely clicked the seat belt when Lou cranked the wheel and dropped the car in gear. The world as I knew it became a cloud of blue smoke. He drove straight up the double-yellow line, engine screaming. *Mufflers howling.* I clawed the sides of my seat on the straightaways, braced myself against the dash on the turns. We came up on another Toyota headed up the hill with a Bush/Quayle bumper sticker. Lou swung into the oncoming lane and I caught a glimpse of an old lady with her white hair in a bun, shaking her head as we zipped by, passing on a blind turn. When we reached the summit, Lou pitched onto the rock road and dropped down into the meadow. MacLeod popped up from the engine compartment of a newer-looking Honda and watched us skid to a stop.

"Got something for you, Mac," said Lou, leaning out the driver window.

MacLeod stood with a wrench in his hand, eyes red as crayon wax. A new lesion had erupted on the bridge of his nose and he pawed it with the back of his hand.

"That a Celica?" he asked.

"Sure is," said Lou. "You can have it for two hundo."

MacLeod bared his horrific teeth, scanning the car with the hyper-eyed look of a sick racoon.

"It's in good shape. What's the catch, Lou?"

"The catch is you stop what the fuck you're doing and break it down right now. Torch the VINS and melt the plates. Bury the carcass. The rest is yours."

"Sounds like I'm the one doing you a favor," he said.

Lou didn't like the reply.

"Do you want it, or not?" His face grew red, a heavy scowl hammered across his forehead. "Or should I take it somewhere else?"

"Fine, yeah, leave it. The boy gonna help me break it down?"

Lou sidled his eyes at me.

"No, I need to keep a close eye on him today."

"What's wrong with him? Looks like he's seen a ghost."

"Maybe he has," said Lou.

He cut the motor and worked the ignition key off the key ring and tossed the remaining keys into a smoldering burn barrel. I thought about all the doors those keys would never open again. The school office. Halbert's home. Who now waited behind those doors? A person passes through certain doorways only so many times and the last one Halbert passed through was my own. My emotions quickly turned to anger. As MacLeod dropped us off in his flatbed truck and paid Lou for the

Toyota, I started to hate Halbert for finding me on that bus stop, for bringing me back home. He'd still be alive and who knows where I'd be by now. One thing I knew for sure: there wasn't a single bus stop or metro station in the entire state of California—no matter the weather or time of day or night—worse than my own home.

Lou marched me into the backyard, the light in the sky just starting to fade. Long shadows reeled over the grass. Maisy stood waist-deep in the hole. The lonely tick and scrape of the shovel might as well have been the only sound left in the world. Halbert had attracted a small cloud of insects now, all of them spinning greedily in a frenzy around his head.

Lou assessed her progress.

"I thought you'd be done by now," he said.

She leaned the shovel against the rim of the grave. Blisters welled from her palms, fingers shaking.

"It's rocky here," she said. "My hands are shot."

He gave the hole another once over.

"It's deep enough. Go ahead and roll him in."

I helped Maisy up and we slid the tarp to the edge of the grave. Halbert's skin had reddened in the sun. There were black marks on his throat where Lou had strangled him with the trimmer line. Together, we rolled him onto his side. He lay like that for a moment, in repose, as if considering the eternity of that dark place before him. Lou came up behind us and gave him a hard kick and he fell away.

"Now bury him," said Lou. "Then dig another grave."

We froze.

"Why another grave?" I asked.

"I told you there'd be a punishment." He slid the revolver from the back of his pants and tipped out the

111

cylinder, gazed one-eyed at the loaded chambers. "You made me kill Cowboy, made me kill that principal fella. If it weren't for the two of you I wouldn't be in this mess. Now dig and make it deep enough for the both of you."

"Don't kill us, Lou," I said. "We didn't have nothing to do with it."

Lou thumbed the cylinder shut and aimed the gun at me.

"You know what I think? I think you've been trying to get rid of me from the start. I think you've been setting me up this whole goddamn time. Trying to send me to the clink, haven't you?"

Maisy had her hands in the air now.

"Please, Lou," she said. "Ben's right, we've been good, just minding our own business."

Lou shook his head.

"Just shut up. I can shoot you now, or shoot you later. Do you want to dig, or do you want to die?"

We picked up our shovels and sorted the loose dirt into the grave. Lou took another long piss on the Grandfather tree and went for the glass pipe on his tool box. He watched us dig for a minute or two, standing in a cloud of his own making, then he wandered back down and lit a cigarette. He sat in his chair, smoking and fidgeting with the cowboy gun. His jaw kept working side to side and every so often he'd bare his teeth at the sky and mumble something we couldn't make out. It looked like he'd entered a world full of things only he could see and hear, and those things tormented him.

Maisy got close enough to whisper in my ear.

"I talked to Mama," she said. "While you were gone."

"What did you say?"

"I told her everything. I told her we needed help."

"I don't see her helping."

"She's gaining strength, Ben. I think I finally got through to her."

I studied the house, stark evening light on the rooftop. A raven perched on the chimney top, dipping its long black neck. The house had never looked so rundown and vacant, as if no one had ever lived there to begin with. A swatch of dry moss hung from the eaves where the sunlight never reached. Paint curling down to the bare naked wood. I imagined Mama watching from the window, the gravity of the scene slowly dawning on her as her children dug their own graves. Motherly instincts ramping up—*taking over.*

Maybe she finally called the police.

Maybe she found some other way.

But I doubted it.

"I don't think she's coming, Maze," I said, my voice breaking up. A sad and hopeless feeling started to take over. It occurred to me that I'd never see Maisy or Mama again, and even though I'd be dead and couldn't care about anything, it brought a crushing feeling of loneliness. I wondered if our ghosts could ever find each other again out here in the dark redwoods. Worse yet, I wondered if he'd shoot Maisy first, and I'd have to see it. The thought was making me crazy, making my whole body shake.

"She'll come, Ben. And that's not all. I have a backup plan."

"Goddamn it, keep shoveling," Lou barked. "I know you're whispering."

It took another twenty minutes to fill Halbert's grave. I did most of the shoveling, and I could see blood darkening the handle of Maisy's shovel. Hands all torn apart.

Tears streamed down her face, gathering at her nose. With each shovel load it seemed that she lost hope, too. I wondered if we could turn on him with the shovels. Maybe he'd only have time to shoot one of us. Maybe one would survive. One of us getting away would be better than none at all.

I broke ground on the second grave, pressed the blade into the earth with the heel of my shoe. The ground was softer here, and Maisy had an easier time with it, too. I nudged her gently.

"We need to fight him," I whispered.

"He'll shoot us. Wait for Mama. I told you I have a plan."

"She's not coming. We have to do it now. Or we run."

She closed her eyes for a long moment. Maybe she'd realized I was right.

She stopped digging and choked up on the shovel.

I choked up on mine.

"Wait," she said. "Keep digging."

"Maze."

"She's coming."

I caught a glimpse, just a quick and fleeting glimpse. There was movement at the back door of the house. I dug. I dug loud, kicking the blade hard into the dirt, trying to mask the sound of her footsteps as she came down the grade. Maisy did the same, even though it hurt her more. I tried not to look, but I couldn't help keeping her in my periphery. She came like a ghost, floating over the dead grass.

Closer now.

Was that a gun in her hand?

"That's enough, Lou," said Mama. "You overstayed your welcome."

Lou jolted in his seat.

Mama leveled a silver pistol in the air. She looked half-dead, like a hospital patient who had just torn the IV tubes from her arms and wandered out the front lobby and onto the street. Sweating and swaying. Ragged hair catching slightly in the breeze. She held the gun two-handedly, feet spaced at shoulder width. Her hips rocked slightly as if finding her balance.

Lou started to rise.

"Drop that gun, Lou," she said. "Drop it and leave."

"Damn, Carolyn," said Lou. "I thought we were friends."

"You know what you are to me."

"Carolyn." He held onto the gun, eyes like tiny blue flames. "You'll be turning tricks for dope. You'll die without me."

"I'll get clean, Lou. I'm going to do it for them."

Lou thought this was funny.

"You don't give a shit about them. You said so yourself. Said you'd sell them both for a fistful of dope next time you were empty."

Mama fired a warning shot into the treetops and we all flinched. I never knew she owned a gun, never even heard a pistol up close until then.

"Does it look like I don't give a shit?" she said.

"Okay, you win," said Lou. "I was gonna leave anyhow."

"After you tied up your loose ends?" Mama spat and motioned with the gun. "You've done enough damage, Lou. For the last time, goddammit, drop it and go."

"You're the boss," he said. He lowered the revolver to the ground, but paused just before it touched the grass. He had a strange smile I'd never seen before, like maybe he'd just calculated his odds and thought they looked good.

He stood up fast, dropped his shoulder.

Mama fired.

Lou's gun flipped into the air. He howled and pulled his hand to his chest. Blood fountained over his arm and stained his shirt. It spurted into the grass all around him. He looked over his hand in a panic, then toed at the dirt.

"You shot my damn finger off, Carolyn!"

"You're lucky," she said, coldly. "I was aiming for your stomach."

Lou cried out *oh dear Lord Jesus* over and over and collected his finger, cradling it gently in his palm. He gave us a crazy look and scurried up the grade toward the side yard, but before he disappeared, he turned and professed to the trees and heavens and all the creatures in the forest that he'd come back for us and that we'd all die slowly for what we'd done to him. Then we heard that godawful truck engine, mud tires squealing onto the road.

We ran to Mama and threw our arms around her.

"I'm so sorry, little ones. I'm so sorry for all of it."

"He was lying, wasn't he, Mama?" said Maisy. "About what you said?"

Mama kneeled. She looked us sharply in the eye. "You know I've been sick. Pretty much all summer long. Lou made me this way. One thing you got to know is that I'm going to get sicker, maybe by tonight. I might even need you to take care of me for a few days. But I'm going to get better and better. I'll be your mama again."

"And no more Lou flu?" I said.

"*Lou flu?*"

"That's what we've been calling it when you get sick."

She shook her head.

"No, kiddo. No more Lou flu."

"You think he's really coming back, like he said?"

Mama looked that way, thoughtfully.

We all did, as if expecting that loud engine to come roaring back into the driveway.

Instead, we heard something else. The skirling sounds of tires on blacktop, followed by a low rumble in the trees. A dozen crows launched into the sky and passed overhead. We huddled together, listening and watching. A curl of gray smoke wound through the tree-tops. It grew thicker, darker. Soon, the plume turned black, roiling at the sky.

"Go inside, sweeties," said Mama. "We're going to have company."

We heard the sirens a few minutes later. Fire trucks roared up and down the road. Next came the Sheriff cruisers. We watched it all from the driveway. After a few hours, the smoke turned gray again, then white. The air smelled like campfire and burnt rubber. Just before sunset, we got a knock on the door. Mama answered. She'd already started getting sick again like she'd told us she would. A Sheriff's deputy asked her about an F-250 and they talked about what color it was and about Lou Holt. He asked about Lou's family and how he might get ahold of his dentist if he had one. The deputy wrote some of what she said down and when he ran out of questions, he told Mama he was sorry and handed her a business card. When he left, Mama collapsed on the couch. She had us bring her a glass of ice water and after she took a sip, she whispered that Lou Holt was never coming back again.

17

"GET DRESSED."

Maisy stood over me as I lay in bed. I blinked, rubbed my eyes. I couldn't read her expression in the dark. She wore a beanie and a jacket, backpack cinched tight over her shoulders.

"Are you running away?" I asked.

"No," she said. "But I want you to come with me."

"Where?"

"Just come."

I dressed quickly and followed close behind, tiptoeing down the hallway. Mama lay moaning and retching until well-past midnight, and now the house felt eerily quiet. Maisy took my hand and led me out the back door. We crossed the yard, past Lou's tool shed and the Grandfather tree. We wandered through the makeshift graveyard and out to the creekbed. She clicked on a flashlight and we regarded the patch of forget-me-nots circling Jessie Barton's grave.

"What are we doing, Maisy?" I whispered.

"Not here," she said, breath steaming. "Just a little farther."

"What about coyotes?"

"They'll leave us alone, I promise."

I rubbed my eyes again. *Was I dreaming?*

I smelled the mineral-laden creek water, breathed the cold mountain air. I rubbed my hands together and felt blisters in the tender cups of my palms.

It was no dream.

We stepped along the banks of the creek until we reached the place where the water deepened. The moon glittered through a break in the tree canopy, its reflection floating on the water like torn cloth. She took my hand, and for a moment I wondered if she expected me to jump into the creek.

"I have a secret, Ben."

I still couldn't read her.

"What kind of secret?"

"It's one that I want you to be a part of, so it'll be a secret we share."

"Okay," I said. "I promise not to tell."

She unshouldered the backpack and set it at her feet.

It sounded full of marbles.

Then she unzipped the front pouch.

"Open your hand," she said.

I held out my hand, palm up. She placed something there, something cold. Something round and metal with a little weight to it. She pinched her fingers in the air, showing one of her own.

A lug nut.

"Go ahead," she said, grinning. "Throw it in."

I looked it over for a long minute, then tossed it into the deep pool. It made a tiny aquatic chime when it hit the water. Ringlets formed and grew until they lapped the tips of our tennis shoes. She threw hers and handed me another from the backpack. We took turns, one after

119

another. Maybe a dozen, maybe more. After we'd tossed in all the lug nuts, she revealed the tire iron and the breaker bar.

"I told you I had a plan," she said, letting it fall with a splash.

"How'd you do it all by yourself?"

"Maybe I'm getting stronger, Ben. Maybe we both are." She put a hand on my shoulder and spat into the water. "So long, Lou. Good riddance."

"So long, Lou," I said, and spat.

As we wound along the creek toward home, Maisy told me a story about Lou Holt emerging from the fiery wreckage of his F-250 in ghostly form, crawling up the scrubby grade with his smoldering beard and scorched blue eyes, hand over hand, only to find Jessie Barton, Cowboy, and Don Halbert, all waiting for him on the shoulder of the road, eyes aglow and phantom claws eager to drag him back down into the flames.

Over and over and so it goes.

EPILOGUE

WE MEET AT THE OAK STREET DINER on a rain-soaked Tuesday morning in November. Nobody recognizes us and no one looks familiar. Most of the folks we'd known left town years ago with each graduation, each marriage, each prison sentence.

Most, but not all.

Some remain buried in that hard mountain clay.

I spot Maisy in the corner booth. She's changed. Sunken features and sharp angles now smoothed over. Worried eyes now calm. Her face brightens when she sees me. She hugs me hard and my first thought is how strong she's become. But she was always strong in other ways, and in those ways much stronger than me.

"You had me worried, brother," she says, looking me over.

"Sometimes I scare myself," I admit. Something about seeing her again brings back a flood of emotions. Tears build in my eye corners. I can't hide them. I know in my heart it's not just her I've missed, but also the woman she has grown to resemble. The woman who raised us and loved us before Lou Holt ruined our lives.

She grabs me by the shoulders.

"Hey, it's me," she says. "We're here to fix things. It'll get better, I promise."

It's warm in the diner, but I don't take off my sweatshirt.

I don't want her to see the abscess in the crook of my arm, the scars and scabs that run down to my wrist like a pegboard.

There's a blonde in the booth where Maisy was sitting. Pretty. Mousey ears. She has a warm smile and gemstone eyes.

"Is this who you told me about?" I ask.

Maisy waves the blonde out of her seat and the two of them intertwine their fingers.

"Yes, this is Megan."

I try to shake her hand, but she hugs me instead.

Megan tells me about the treatment center she works at in San Jose, how it's one of the best in the state. She tells me she has a good feeling about me and how she has a knack for predicting treatment outcomes. I ask about the cost and she shrugs it off.

"I guess that's another reason we're here, Ben."

I take a deep, shuddering breath. I haven't scored in a day and a half and I feel like I'm dying. Every nerve in my body tells me to bolt out the front door.

Maisy glances at her phone.

"It's almost time," she says. "Do you want coffee?"

I nod. If it were anyone else, I'd be long gone. Anyone but her.

Sergeant Munro arrives a few minutes later. He introduces himself, eyeing me suspiciously the way cops do. Maybe he'd looked up my record already. Maybe it was instinct. He probably deals with guys like me every day.

He doesn't squeeze into the booth with us. Instead, he grabs a loose chair and settles it at the head of the table.

Maisy unfolds two slips of paper and lays them down.

"I've held onto these for years," she says.

One is the missing persons flyer for Jessie Barton.

The other is for Don Halbert.

Munro tells us the families are still willing to honor the rewards, but he folds his arms when he says it, like we're holding the information ransom. He tells us some people talk out of the kindness of their hearts.

The table grows quiet.

"We're not greedy," I say. "One thing Don Halbert taught me is that it's okay to ask for help. Sometimes it's the only way through. This time, the help goes both ways."

"My brother and I have been through a lot, Sergeant Munro," says Maisy. "We're just a couple of foster kids who almost didn't make it. My brother's right. We could use all the help we can get."

The waitress brings a round of coffee and Munro takes a careful sip without adding cream or sugar.

"Okay," he says. "The thing that surprises me here, if I'm being perfectly honest, is that we still get tips every once in a while for the Barton girl. A sighting here and there. Most are wingnuts looking for long-shot reward money. Maybe all of them are. But I haven't had a tip about Don Halbert in ten years. You can see why I'm skeptical."

"I get it," I say. "But we know where he is."

"How do you know?"

"Because we buried him up Bear Creek Road twelve years ago."

"And you buried Jessie Barton, too?"

"No," says Maisy. "Lou did."

Munro straightens in his seat as if a jolt had run up his spine.

"Lou?"

"Lou Holt."

He takes a sharp breath and stares out the rain-spattered window.

Outside, a mud-stained woman appears and presses into the glass, trying to escape the weather. She finds a half-smoked cigarette on the brick ledge and lights it, takes a drag. Her hands shake. She peers through the window, staring down at us like we're living in another time and place. Another dimension. A little plume of tobacco smoke spreads over the glass and she turns around, cinches the collar of her tattered jacket, and watches the street.

"Lou Holt, huh?" says Munro. He plays it cool, looking at his hands, picking at his fingernails. I can tell that he knows the name. It means something to him. "Tell me more about him. Let's start from the beginning."

ACKNOWLEDGMENTS

I would like to acknowledge the debt I owe to the writers and editors who have encouraged me over the years: Meagan Lucas, Suz Jay, Rob Smith, Curtis Ippolito, Stephen J. Golds, Zakariah Johnson, Russell Johnson, J.B. Stevens, Coy Hall, D.T. Neal, Catherine McCarthy, John Kojak, Chris McGinley, and Rebecca Rowland, to name a few. They say writing is a lonely business, but I have found this to be untrue.

Thanks also to Ron Earl Phillips for your support and patience, and for making this book possible.

C.W. Blackwell is an American author from the Central Coast of California. His recent work has appeared with *Down and Out Books*, *Shotgun Honey*, *Tough Magazine*, and *Reckon Review*. He is a 2021 Derringer award winner and 2022 Derringer finalist. His debut fiction novella ***Song of the Red Squire*** was published in 2022 from *Nosetouch Press*.

SHOTGUN HONEY

2012 • 2022

CELEBRATING 10 YEARS OF
FICTION WITH A KICK

THE ROAD IS JUST BEGINNING
shotgunhoneybooks.com

CPSIA information can be obtained
at www.ICGtesting.com
Printed in the USA
BVHW042240180123
656596BV00023B/235